'How About It, Jess?'

Gareth smiled. 'Shall we console each other?'

'Would you care to elaborate on this "proposition" of yours?'

'I'm suggesting dinner together. Tonight. And afterwards . . . whatever you care for.'

'Supposing,' she said suspiciously, 'what I care for is to go home and go to bed . . . alone?'

'Whatever you like. So are we having dinner together, or do I consult my little black book?'

'Okay,' she said at last, feeling reckless. 'Why not?'

LAUREY BRIGHT

has held a number of different jobs, but has never wanted to be anything but a writer. She lives in New Zealand, where she creates the stories of contemporary people in love that have won her a following all over the world.

Dear Reader:

Romance readers have been enthusiastic about Silhouette Special Editions for years. And that's not by accident: Special Editions were the first of their kind and continue to feature realistic stories with heightened romantic tension.

The longer stories, sophisticated style, greater sensual detail and variety that made Special Editions popular are the same elements that will make you want to read book after book.

We hope that you enjoy this Special Edition today, and will enjoy many more.

The Editors at Silhouette Books

LAUREY BRIGHT
Fetters of the Past

Silhouette Special Edition

Published by Silhouette Books New York

America's Publisher of Contemporary Romance

SILHOUETTE BOOKS

Copyright © 1985 by Laurey Bright
Cover artwork copyright © 1985 Franco Accornero

Distributed by Pocket Books

ISBN: 0-373-09002-1

First Silhouette Books printing January, 1985

10 9 8 7 6 5 4 3 2 1

Map by Ray Lundgren

America's Publisher of Contemporary Romance

Printed in the U.S.A.

Silhouette Books by Laurey Bright

Fetters of the Past

Chapter One

 ess sat in a window seat, ignoring the chatter in the big room as she twisted her body to look out at the harbour, its water diamond-sprinkled by teasing spring sunshine, and watch the pleasure craft sailing smoothly in the stiff breeze or riding at anchor in the bay.

Around the shoreline an occasional splash of yellow wattle in full bloom contrasted with the deep blue of the sea, and beyond its sheltering arms lay the sturdy arch of the Bridge and the distant multistoreyed buildings of the business centre on the opposite side of the harbour. From this luxury penthouse overlooking Lavender Bay, Pietro Benotti enjoyed one of the best views in Sydney.

She heard Pietro's pleased laughter rising above the other voices and smiled a little. She liked the wealthy Italian-Australian. And he was having a marvellous time launching Claire, his once long-lost stepdaughter, into marriage, only regretting the fact that he had been able to have her living with him and his two grown sons for such a short time before Scott Carver had snatched her up to be his wife.

Jess looked across the room crowded with wedding guests—two wine waiters circulating among them—and found Pietro, dark and distinguished, standing by Scott and Claire, his hand on the bridegroom's arm, his beaming gaze fixed on his stepdaughter. Claire looked suitably radiant in a gown of cream antique lace, trimmed at the waist and the modestly scooped neckline with rows of silk forget-me-nots. The same flowers adorned her fair hair in a dainty wreath.

Her eyes leaving the bridal party, Jess idly scanned the groups of people standing or sitting about with glasses in their hands, scraps of conversation floating to her ears: '. . . pretty wedding . . . so lucky to have a nice day for it . . . handsome, isn't he? Love that tall, blond, broad-shouldered look . . . and such a beautiful bride . . . Pietro found her in a convent . . . the little flower girls are from the orphanage . . . so sweet . . . Scott's a lucky man . . .'

Yes, you are, friend, she thought, and returned her gaze to Scott where he stood with his arm proudly encircling the waist of his very new wife. He was looking down at Claire with an expression that sent a pang through Jess, and her mouth turned down a little bitterly for a moment before Scott looked up and met her eyes with a vividly blue glance. With her glass of champagne, she toasted them silently. Claire, talking to Jonnie, her teenage half brother, didn't notice. But Scott nodded an acknowledgement before his attention reverted to the sparklingly happy young woman at his side.

Reminding herself that envy was an emotion that soured one's disposition, Jess sipped some more of the champagne, shifted restlessly and began to look about again, her lids drooping indolently over shimmering emerald green eyes, her body relaxed against the cushions in the corner of the window seat, giving an impression of elegant boredom.

Suddenly she found herself arrested by a face that she knew, an ice-blue gaze, much colder than Scott's, that seemed to pierce her like a stiletto. Her lips parted on a sharply indrawn breath, and although she didn't move, every muscle tightened imperceptibly like a violin string being adjusted to a more perfect pitch. She dropped her eyes quickly, then raised them again to give Gareth Seymour a polite little nod of recognition that she hoped would conform with the conventions while conveying a definite message that she didn't want to have him come over and speak to her.

Even as she turned rather pointedly back to the window, she knew that he was on his way to her side. The carpet was too thick and the conversation in the room too noisy for her to have heard him, but she was acutely aware of his every movement until he stood only inches away. He looked over her head at the view, then down at the short, softly shining dark hair brushed back in feathery wings from her temples and sleekly moulded to the shape of the head that remained stubbornly averted from him.

He didn't speak, and her taut nerves at last made it impossible for her to ignore him any longer. She turned without haste, her face blank, her carefully shaped eyebrows arching as she met his cool stare.

His lips moved in a restrained possibility of a smile.

'Here's to *déja vu,*' he said quietly, having gained her attention, and raised his glass to her.

'I don't know what you mean,' she lied. 'But I'm willing to drink to anything, provided it doesn't compromise me.' Her low, smoky voice, imbued with humour, didn't falter.

He leaned on the frame of the window. Although the seat would have been big enough for two, the full skirt of her amber silk dress was spread across the squab, and her sideways position, with her long, slim legs in their sheer stockings neatly crossed, was a 'keep away' signal. She was relieved that he had respected it.

'Don't you?' he said, referring to the first part of her reply. His eyes challenged her, but when she declined to give him an answer he didn't pursue it.

She lifted her brows again in apparent tolerant puzzlement, but, unable to withstand his rapier glance, she made an excuse of her drink and bent her head to sip at it.

When they first met she had been sitting alone—no, she amended, not alone, with a group of people—but lonely, holding a glass of champagne or something else. She didn't remember now, but it had been some kind of wine. And she had looked up and met that same passionless, appraising glance, too analytical for comfort. She had stared back, expecting him to look away, but he hadn't. She had found it very disconcerting. He had made her equally uncomfortable each time they met since. She refused to count the number—perhaps half a dozen times. She wouldn't grant him that much importance in her life.

The first time she had seen him—that wasn't strictly true either, she supposed. Only minutes before she had been talking to him and Claire, but seeing him only as

Claire's date for the evening, someone who had lent her a pen to write down the address of the friend she had lost touch with and had been delighted to find again. She had taken little interest in him then, except to wonder if Claire was serious about him, deciding quite quickly that by all the signs she wasn't. Then after returning to her own table, she had looked up and found him *inspecting* her, not looking with admiration or warm speculation in the way she was accustomed to from men, but with a chilling detachment, a clinical and almost frightening observation, as though he were a scientist confronted with a new life form.

It was odd that initially he had made almost no impression on her, and yet on every subsequent occasion she had been unable to ignore him. She hadn't even remembered his name after Claire's introduction, had needed to ask him for it again on their second meeting, but she had certainly known who he was and where she had seen him before, and been surprised to recognise the sexual antagonism crackling between them. Sometimes she wondered if he did it on purpose, if he had been piqued by her total lack of awareness in those first few minutes of their acquaintance and had made up his mind it shouldn't happen again.

And yet there was no overt deliberation on his part. He had none of the obvious sexual tactics of the predatory male. His features were lean and regular and added up to average looks, except for the slight shock of a direct glance from those deceptively sharp eyes. And at close quarters his rather thin mouth had a chiselled look. He was above average height, not as tall as Scott, but topping Jess's five-eight by a few inches, and he wouldn't have won a body-building competition, though he couldn't by any stretch of the imagination have been classed as weedy. He moved with an unobtrusive masculine grace, and had a quality of stillness which could be disconcerting, and yet she had no doubt at all that when necessary he could snap to instant attention.

His clothes were in quiet good taste and well fitting, not at all flamboyant, nor apparently calculated to arouse feminine interest, but even the grey suit, charcoal tie and self-striped pale blue shirt which he wore today added indefinably to the understated urbanity of his personality.

Her glass was nearly empty, and she was unable to pretend an absorbed interest in the champagne any longer. She had to look up, half aware even as she did so that her reluctance made the slow, upward sweep of her lashes languorously seductive.

Wasted on him, of course. The steady gaze didn't flicker, and she felt a prickle of annoyance as she met it. She was looking her best today. The bronze dress emphasised the colour of her eyes and her clear tanned skin. Her makeup had been carefully applied to complement the dress: mascara and eyeshadow to highlight her best feature, light foundation worn without powder, just a hint of a flattering blusher on her cheekbones and glossy lipstick outlining a mouth which she had been told often enough was delectably feminine. For all the effect it had on Gareth Seymour, she might have been wearing sackcloth and ashes. He had a knack of shaking her self-confidence, and she didn't like that.

She finished her drink in a gulp and was about to get up, glad of the excuse to leave him. But before she could even murmur, 'I want another drink,' he had swooped forward without any appearance at all of haste and taken the glass neatly from her hand.

'I'll get it,' he told her, standing in front of her so that she was effectively stopped from rising.

'Thank you.' She smiled as sweetly as she knew how, thinking that it would give her an opportunity to escape while he made his way to the bar in the next room.

To her chagrin, however, he merely turned and raised a hand, snapping his fingers confidently, and in two seconds one of the waiters stood before them with a loaded tray.

As Gareth thanked the man and passed her a full glass, she reflected bitterly that she should have expected it.

What was more, she realised with dismay, her movement had effectively left half of the window seat empty and Gareth was calmly seating himself beside her.

There was plenty of room, and even as she eased unobtrusively away from him to lean once more into the corner cushions, he was doing the same at the other end, regarding her with a slight curve to his mouth, making no attempt to sit close, his arm resting casually along the ledge of the windowsill.

He raised his glass silently to her in a rather mocking way, and, pretending nonchalance, she did the same, with a twist of her own mouth.

'You didn't cry in church,' he said unexpectedly.

'What?'

'It's a feminine prerogative, isn't it? I noticed a few handkerchiefs coming out. But you were quite dry-eyed.'

He'd been watching her? A reluctant thrust of suppressed excitement passed through her.

'It would ruin my mascara,' she said succinctly.

He smiled. 'That argues a certain amount of will-power.'

'So?' She stared at him coldly. Was he suggesting she was lacking in that?

He moved his head slightly, acknowledging that the thought had crossed his mind, amused at her annoyance. 'Did you *want* to cry?' he asked softly. His eyes left hers for a moment to find Scott and Claire, who were circulating among their guests, both of them flushed with happiness, and then returned to her face, waiting for a reply.

She was certain Claire had never been in love with him, but she was not so sure of Gareth's feelings. She didn't know him well, and he was very good at hiding any hint of emotion. Curious, and with malice aforethought, she said, 'Did *you?*'

His smile deepened, his eyes never wavering from hers. 'Not particularly. Do you always answer with a question?'

She shrugged. 'If it seems relevant.'

'I don't see the relevance in this instance.' Lawyer's talk, his voice very dry.

Jess said, 'I thought you might have been crossed in love.' Certainly Pietro had at one time regarded Gareth as a serious rival to Scott for his stepdaughter's affections. She watched him for his reaction, a pulse in her throat jumping erratically.

He didn't move a muscle, his expression giving nothing away except perhaps a faint, wary curiosity of his own. 'I wonder why you should think that,' he said very softly. She was suddenly aware that he had a really beautiful voice, not too deep, but with a velvety masculine intonation that was sending a responsive quiver down her spine.

Alarmed by this symptom of susceptibility, she said

almost sharply, 'Isn't it obvious? You were with Claire the first time I met you—'

'Ah!' he interrupted, in exaggerated surprise. 'You do remember?'

She felt sudden warmth beneath the blusher on her cheeks. 'You were certainly dating her before Scott came back into the picture . . . and for a while afterwards.'

'And that's it?' he asked with calm scorn. As she remained silent, he said, 'Contrary to your rather overblown romantic fantasies, I don't necessarily fall madly in love with every pretty girl I happen to take out a few times.'

Smarting under the sarcasm, she said shortly, 'I didn't suppose so. You were the one who made the crack about crying in church.'

His eyes gleamed for a moment with something— perhaps amusement or anger, she wasn't sure. 'To that I plead guilty,' he said with spurious humility. 'Small talk,' he explained. 'It leads down some interesting bypaths, doesn't it? You haven't answered my question, though.'

'You didn't answer mine,' she shot back.

This time the gleam was definitely one of appreciation. When his eyes did lose their guarded coldness, they were really remarkably expressive. He looked at her steadily, as though weighing something up. Then he said, 'I might have asked her to marry me if Scott hadn't come back into her life. And I think that she might have accepted. She's a lovely girl, and I'm glad she's happy.' He still wasn't giving much away, but the inference was obvious. He had wanted to marry Claire. It had been, on his part, that serious. . . . Well, she had asked—and for some reason his answer had given her a strange, hollow sensation in her stomach. . . .

He started to say something else, and she thought he was going to demand an answer to his own question, but Scott and Claire had reached them in their slow progress among the guests, and good manners forced him to his feet to shake the groom's hand and demand the traditional kiss from the bride.

It was only a light peck, Jess noticed as she too stood, her high heels bringing her almost on a level with Gareth as he stepped back, smiling down at Claire's upturned, laughing face. He obviously had his feelings well under control.

She returned Scott's casual 'Hello.' And the knowledge hit her that their relationship from this day on had changed irrevocably. Theirs had been a special friendship for which she had reason to be grateful, and it had lasted a long time, but now he belonged to Claire. Things would never be quite the same.

'We'll be off soon,' he said. 'Thanks for coming, Jess. It's good to see you. And thanks for the present, whatever it is.' He grinned.

'I didn't buy you one,' she told him, grinning back, at the same moment that Claire said, 'A hand-painted Chinese dinner set, and it's gorgeous. Thank you, Jess.'

'Bless you,' Jess said lightly, leaning over to kiss her cheek. 'Enjoy it, and I hope you have a wonderful honeymoon and a wonderful married life.'

She turned to Scott and felt tears unexpectedly stinging behind her eyes. 'And you,' she said huskily, taking his hand. 'Good-bye, good luck.'

She saw the flicker of surprised understanding in his eyes and felt the pressure of his fingers on hers, and on impulse she lifted her face and kissed him on the mouth, her lips pressed for a few seconds against the answering warmth of his.

They were both smiling when they parted, but she caught a set look on Claire's face and put out a hand to clasp her arm, her eyes saying reproachfully, *Silly! It's nothing to worry about.* And she was relieved to see Claire smile back the message, *I know. Sorry.*

Claire had not been a part of Scott's and Jess's world, where kisses were casually exchanged and relationships were fluid. But she was secure enough now in Scott's love and Jess's friendship to know that whatever the kiss meant to them, it was not a threat to her happiness.

Someone caught at Scott's sleeve, and the newlyweds turned to speak to him. Jess's eyes were misty and stinging, and the shock of hard fingers encircling her arm in a painful grip made her gasp, the still unshed tears trembling dangerously on her lower lashes.

'Come with me!' Gareth's voice was low and strangely angry, and because she couldn't see well she let him lead her out through a narrow door onto a small balcony overlooking the water. 'Here,' he said, thrusting a square of linen into her hand. 'Use this.'

But the breeze coming off the sea was already drying the tears, and she swallowed twice and took a deep breath, looking steadfastly out at the multicoloured sails of the yachts dancing on the glittering surface of the bay, determined that she wasn't going to cry. After a few minutes she raised one hand and surreptitiously wiped her fingers carefully over the dampness under her eyes, then thrust Gareth's handkerchief back at him. 'I don't need it,' she said distantly, looking defiantly into his eyes.

He was frowning, and there was a tightness about his mouth. Odd that Gareth should be one of those men who couldn't bear to see a woman cry. She supposed that after his fashion he had been kind. He must be relieved that she wasn't, after all, going to soak his handkerchief or demand the comfort of a masculine shoulder on which to pour her tears. No one else could even have noticed, but he had been standing so close and had certainly been thoughtful or at least resourceful in whisking her away to the only nearby privacy available.

'Sorry,' she said, smiling in self-mockery. 'It's a little difficult to explain.'

'Don't try,' he said curtly. 'I have my answer, I think.'

For a moment she didn't know what he meant. Then, pride coming to the fore, she gave a scornful little laugh and said, 'Look, I'm not suffering from a broken heart!'

'No,' he said sardonically. 'Of course not.'

She made a helpless, frustrated gesture with her hands. 'Scott and I are old friends. . . .'

'So I believe.' His voice sounded clipped. 'What kind of friends?'

About to protest, *'Just friends!'* she remembered the few occasions when friendship had become something warmer and more intimate, and felt a betraying heat rise to her cheeks. It was the second time in fifteen minutes that he had made her blush, and she was long past the age for it. How could she adequately describe a relationship as long and complicated as hers and Scott's to this man who was almost a stranger to them both?

And why should she? Defensively she said, 'You don't understand, and anyway, I don't owe you any explanations.'

'Right on the second count, at any rate,' he answered. 'You're shivering. Shall we go inside?'

She thought he would leave her once he had found her another drink, but he didn't. He stayed by her side, took the empty glass from her as she finished, and when Jonnic called that his half-sister and Scott were leaving, and the guests made their way out to the street to see them off, he insisted on their going down together. 'Claire will want you there,' he said tersely when she protested that it wasn't necessary to join the crowd on the steps of the apartment building. Apparently what Claire wanted he was determined to see she got. Probably, she realised, it was for Claire's sake that he had seemed annoyed by her tears.

The bridal couple appeared, running the gamut of confetti-throwing well-wishers, and made for the waiting car. But as Scott held the door for her, Claire turned, bouquet in hand, and searched among the crowd. Jess met her eyes, and her mouth silently formed the word 'No!' but Claire, smiling gaily, had already hurled the flowers before being helped into the car by Scott.

Her aim was good, but Jess kept her arms rigidly at her sides and tried to step back, only to be brought up short by a hard, masculine body behind her. At the same time Gareth's arms came round her, and he neatly fielded the bouquet and lifted her hand to curl her fingers around the wrapped stalks.

'Yours, I think,' he said in her ear as a few nearby guests cheered and applauded. He removed his arms, and she whirled round to stare at him furiously. He merely raised his brows a fraction and stared right back with an otherwise bland expression. 'Come on,' he said, taking her arm again. 'Let's go back upstairs.'

In the apartment she managed to avoid him by making a beeline for Pietro and engaging him for some time in a spirited conversation. Then someone put on some records and she danced for a time with Jonnie and his brother and some other boys, all at least five years younger than herself, but she enjoyed it, working up a thirst which she quenched with more champagne.

Some time later, as she took another glass from one of the trays, a lean hand deftly removed it from her grasp.

Turning an indignant face to the perpetrator, she saw Gareth Seymour's face swim into sharp focus against a foggy background of other people. 'Haven't you had enough?' he asked quite mildly, his eyes demanding an answer.

Enraged, but compelled to honesty by the direct challenge of his gaze, she sighed and said, 'Yes.' The rest of the room seemed decidedly muzzy and the noise was like waves of sound breaking against her eardrums. But she was still able to dance, and there was nothing wrong with her speech. 'I'm not drunk,' she told him.

'No. But you haven't got far to go, have you?'

He wasn't telling her, he was inviting her to assess her own condition, and the galling thing was that he was perfectly right. Her mouth curving cynically, she gave him the full force of her green gaze. 'Have you appointed yourself my guardian angel?' she demanded.

'No.' He looked at her thoughtfully. 'But I have a proposition to make, and I don't usually make propositions to tipsy ladies.'

Provocatively, she pursed her lips and looked at him sideways with an amused, husky, 'Oh?'

He smiled. 'How about it, Jess? Shall we console each other, now that our two—friends have figuratively ridden off into the sunset together?'

'Fig-ur-at-ively,' she repeated ruminatively. *'You*

have obviously *not* been overimbibing of Pietro's wonderful champagne. Would you care,' she added rather carefully, 'to elaborate on this "proposition" of yours?'

'I'm suggesting dinner together.'

'Tonight?'

'Tonight.'

'And afterwards?'

'And afterwards . . . whatever you care for.'

'Supposing,' she said suspiciously, 'what I care for is to go home and go to bed—alone?'

He shrugged. 'That's fine. Whatever you like.'

Thoughtfully she said, 'I could take that as a slight.'

He laughed at her, the first time she had seen him truly laugh. 'You'll take it whichever way you want to,' he said. 'But are we having dinner together, or do I consult my little black book?'

'Rotter,' she said amiably. Perhaps it was the amount of champagne she had consumed, but something seemed to have dulled the edge of the queer, piquant discomfort that he aroused in her. 'Okay,' she said at last, feeling reckless. 'Why not?'

Chapter Two

'Do you like to eat ethnic?' he asked her as he slid into the driver's seat of the silver-grey Saab after ushering her into the car.

'Yes,' she answered, 'but after all the food at the wedding reception I'm not sure I fancy anything too heavy or spicy.'

'I feel much the same. What about a French crêperie? I know a place that has a good range of fillings, sweet and savoury. It's at Botany Bay, so the drive may give us an appetite. Fancy it?'

'Sounds ideal.'

He started the car and it slid smoothly away from the kerb. Something about the closed-in atmosphere made her overconscious of the brush of his sleeve against her arm as he released the brake, so that she tensed with the effort not to jerk herself away.

For a while he drove in silence, and she gazed out at the passing houses without really seeing them. He turned a corner, passed a slow driver in front of them, then swung onto the bridge approach before he glanced her way.

'Did you enjoy the wedding?' he asked formally.

She should have answered that it had been lovely, everything had gone without a hitch, the bride looked beautiful, the bridegroom was a lucky man. She looked out at the broad sweep of the harbour below, a ferry boat cutting a white swath across its surface with the sail-like multiple roofs of the Opera House beyond it. Shifting restlessly on the dark blue leather seat, she said, 'I find that weddings are to be endured rather than enjoyed.'

He laughed quietly. 'I agree that the formalities can be a bit daunting, but the speeches and toasts today were kept to a sensible minimum, and the ceremony has a certain grace, don't you think? There's something about the marriage ritual that makes even cynics relent a little.'

'Not this cynic.'

'*Are* you one?'

'Are *you?*' she countered.

He paused, seemingly giving the question some serious thought. 'No, I don't think I am.'

'You surprise me. I thought you were a lawyer.'

'How did you know?'

'I guessed,' she told him, looking sideways at him for a reaction, but none came. 'And Claire said yes, you were.'

A flicker of expression crossed his face then, the corners of his mouth curving just a fraction. 'So you were discussing me with Claire.'

That pleased him, she saw, and with a sense of having made a damaging admission, she drawled, 'Actually, I was trying to warn her. Only as it turned out I needn't have. She obviously didn't care at all for you.'

Bitch! she said to herself immediately as the faint smile on his lips disappeared. *Why must you be such a bitch?*

One of the great stone buttresses flashed by, and they passed fleetingly under the dark bar of its shadow on the downward curve of the roadway.

'Why,' Gareth asked evenly, 'did you think it necessary to warn Claire about me?'

'Look, I shouldn't have said that. I'm sorry.'

He looked at her with a hint of surprise. 'Okay. But you did. I know of two reasons why a woman might warn another woman off a man that she's been seeing. Either the first woman wants him herself—which I take it doesn't apply—or she knows something damaging about him. I may not be a saint, but as far as I'm aware my reputation isn't so disreputable that I'd make unsuitable company for an innocent girl.'

'Claire is more innocent than most.'

'Granted. She's spent a large part of her life in a convent environment of one sort or another. But I'm not a lecher.'

'I didn't think that you were. I just didn't want her hurt.'

'I'm sorry,' he said politely. 'I don't follow.'

'Call it instinct,' she suggested, 'born of experience.'

'Since you and I could hardly be said to have any shared experience,' Gareth mused dryly, 'I take it you're referring to your own experience . . . with men in general.'

'That's right.' Her voice had lost its usual smoky softness and the words came out hard and clipped.

He looked at her consideringly, openly appraising her, a deep glint of angry mockery in his eyes. 'Vast, is it?' he suggested gently.

He expected her to flush and turn away, she supposed. Well, she wasn't going to. Keeping her eyes coolly on his face, she said, 'Certainly more so than Claire's.'

'That wouldn't be too difficult. What is it that this superior knowledge of yours tells you about me?'

Jess shrugged. 'You don't want to know.'

'Of course I want to know. You've aroused my curiosity, and you needn't think you'll be let off the hook now.'

'I just didn't think you were her type, that's all.'

'Ah. Because I'm not like Scott?'

'I didn't know then about her and Scott.'

'But you knew—or thought you knew—a whole lot about me. In spite of the fact that we'd barely exchanged two words.'

'I told you . . .'

'Oh, yes. This famous instinct.'

He drove in silence for some time, while the sun lowered and the dusk shadowed the interior of the car. His driving style was assured and competent but never too fast or aggressive. When he had to stop at a traffic signal he turned to her, his eyes light and too uncomfortably penetrating in the glow of a street lamp. 'You might as well tell me,' he said softly, 'how you think you know so much about me.'

'All right,' Jess said indifferently. 'It's all in your eyes. They're cold and cruel . . .'

'*Cruel?*'

'Hard, then,' she amended. 'Unfeeling. Claire

wouldn't have stood a chance against that, if she'd been foolish enough to fall in love with you.'

The signal changed to green and the car moved off, and after a while he said almost absently, 'Then isn't it fortunate that she didn't?'

Jess certainly thought so, but she had a distinct impression that she had pushed her luck far enough. He wasn't showing much on the surface, but intuition told her that underneath he was in a quiet rage. She opened the clutch purse on her lap and said, 'Do you mind if I smoke?'

'If you want to,' he said. 'I can't say I care for the smell of tobacco on a woman's breath.'

With a filter tip held in her fingers, she paused, burning with a rage of her own. 'I promise not to breathe on you,' she said, and placing the cigarette between her lips, took out a discreetly elegant gold lighter and with a perfectly steady hand brought the flame to the end of the cigarette.

She lowered the window a little and blew the thin trail of vapour away from him. 'You don't smoke,' she said. 'How very virtuous.'

'Not virtuous. It's a matter of enlightened self-interest.'

'Have you never smoked?' she enquired carefully.

'When I was very young, of course, I tried it.'

'But you had enough willpower to stop?'

'I had enough sense never to really start. Have you ever tried to stop?'

'Not seriously. No willpower, you see.'

'Or no motivation?'

She took a long draw and let out her breath gently. Smoke wreathed in front of her face, and she opened the window another inch or two. What would he know about motivation? She supposed it was true; she had never cared enough about her health to give up smoking, except for the brief few months when she had stopped completely because the baby's health had also been at risk. . . .

Determined not to think of that, she said, 'Where is this place you're taking me to?'

'Not far now.'

They didn't speak again. At last he turned off the highway and in a few minutes they were outside an unprepossessing building that looked like some kind of public utility. Once inside she found it was a warm and cosy little restaurant and the table they were shown to had a lovely view out over Botany Bay.

'Very nice,' she commented as the waiter went away after taking their order.

'I'm glad you like it. It isn't expensive or fancy, but they have good food and it's fully licensed. I thought a light, sparkling white . . . suit you?'

Jess nodded. 'Thank you.'

She looked out at the view as he ordered the wine. This, she reflected, was where it had all begun, the history of the Europeans in Australia. Botany Bay had been the destination of the First Fleet when it sailed from England in 1787 with a cargo of five hundred and seventy male and less than two hundred female convicts, banished from their homes in Britain to the other side of the earth. She tried to imagine how it had looked then. Governor Phillip had taken one look at Botany Bay and decided that Sydney Cove, a few miles further round the coast, was a more suitable site, but the ships sailing to the largest prison on earth over the next eighty years continued to be known as 'Botany Bay ships.' For many years people with convict forebears had preferred to forget it, but lately, being able to trace one's family to the noisome holds of the First Fleet had become a source of pride. Jess had never bothered to find out about her ancestry.

Gareth hadn't said anything for some minutes. She felt his eyes on her face and made it as expressionless as she could, until at last she could stand the steady scrutiny no longer and turned to look at him accusingly. 'What do you think you're doing?'

'Admiring the view.'

She had fallen straight into that, of course. She knew perfectly well which view he had been looking at, but it wasn't admiration that she saw in his eyes. They were as cool and calculating as ever. She would have taken a bet that he had no reprehensible ancestors. More likely the first Seymour had been one of the administrators— probably an army officer, responsible for enforcing the rigid and brutal discipline of the day on the hapless convicts.

He said, 'Surely you're used to being stared at?'

Not like that! was her involuntary reaction. But she wouldn't give him the satisfaction of knowing that he had unsettled her. She merely raised her left eyebrow very slightly, a trick she had deliberately cultivated, and fumbled in her bag to extract a cigarette.

He put out a hand and lightly caught her wrist. 'I don't really like cigarette smoke mixed with my meal.'

'We haven't got a meal yet.' She was looking down at their hands, his long fingers encircling her wrist, where the pulse beat had just inexplicably quickened.

'It lingers,' he said.

He removed his hand, enabling her to breathe more freely, and very carefully she returned the cigarette to its case and snapped it shut before returning it to the bag. She said, her voice light and brittle, 'Do you usually take a woman out and spend the time criticising her habits?'

'I just stated a preference, that's all. I'd appreciate it if you'd refrain from marring my pleasure in a good meal.'

'Perhaps you'd have enjoyed it more on your own.'

'I hope not. You're very easy on the eyes, and I suspect you can be good company when you like. I'm sorry if I've offended you, but I would have picked you for a person who appreciates straight talking.'

The wine arrived in its bucket of ice, the business of serving it interrupting the flow of conversation, and when the waiter had left Gareth suggested, 'Shall we toast the newlyweds?'

'By all means.' She sipped at the cool, crisp liquid, then put the glass down on the starched tablecloth.

'Don't you like it?' he enquired.

'Yes, but, as you reminded me earlier, I've had a lot of champagne already, and I'm sure you'd hate me to get drunk. I'll wait until there's some food to offset the effects.'

'Very wise. What, as a matter of curiosity, are the likely effects?'

'Of too much drink? I'd probably get either belligerent or . . .'

'Or . . . ?'

One shoulder lifted infinitesimally, her eyes daring his reaction. 'Or amorous.'

He smiled. 'That might be interesting.'

'It might be embarrassing. You wouldn't like that. Even back at the wedding reception, you were anxious for me not to . . . overindulge.'

'Perhaps I just wanted to get you to myself before it all happened.'

'Oh?' She looked at him from under her lashes. 'Does that mean you have nefarious designs on me?'

A smile twitched at his mouth. 'Possibly,' he drawled. 'Would you mind?'

His eyes challenged her, and she tried to quell a quick excitement. 'Sorry,' she said, 'I'm not interested.'

He looked back at her, searching her face. 'Have some more wine,' he invited suggestively, making her laugh.

The crêpes arrived, crisp-edged and delicious: hers filled with smoked salmon and sour cream, and his with a seafood mixture in a smooth sauce. They shared a salad between them and finished with a fruit dessert and coffee.

Gareth lifted the wine bottle, still about a third full, and directed a questioning glance at her. Recklessly she nodded. Why not? The meal had been perfect, and she felt not in the least light-headed, but pleasantly replete and almost sleepy.

He poured half of what was left into her glass, and the rest into his own, lifting it in a silent toast to her.

She picked up her glass and clinked it gently against his, her smile mocking. 'Thanks for the dinner,' she said. 'It was superb.'

'Here's to the next one.' His eyes were watchful as they met hers.

The liquid in her glass trembled, her eyes going down, avoiding his. She didn't answer but swallowed half of her wine in an almost defiant gesture.

She lowered the glass and absently twirled it on the table while he sat back, apparently relaxed, and sipped at the remainder of his wine.

'Coffee, I think?' he queried when he set down the empty glass.

Jess finished her wine quickly and said, 'If you take me home I'll make you some at my place, if you like.'

Briefly he paused, then said, 'Of course I'm taking you home. You don't have a car, do you?'

'No. I don't drive.'

He looked at her oddly, but said nothing as he got up to move her chair.

Her home was a restored colonial cottage, with wrought-iron 'lace' decorating the tiny veranda fronting the quiet street, and a small yard at the back. She had furnished it with a mixture of traditional and modern pieces: the carpet on the floor of the living room a fine, hand-woven oriental rug gleaming with jewel colours, the sofa a genuine antique, the small round coffee table of polished pine an unexpectedly effective contrast. The mantel above the original old fireplace held a variety of ornaments, from a Solomon Islands carving in black wood to a delicate Chinese porcelain plate and an elegantly elongated ceramic Siamese cat; and on the chimney breast hung a number of prints and photographs of old Sydney.

Gareth was examining them when she came in from the tiny kitchen, holding an island-made woven pandanus leaf tray with two pottery mugs of steaming coffee.

'You're interested in history?' he asked her as she put the tray on the table.

'I just thought they'd add a nice decorative note,' she

said, handing him a mug as he strolled over, and indicating the sofa.

He sat down, looking at her thoughtfully, a half smile on his lips. She took her own mug and sat on a buttoned velvet slipper chair opposite.

'You don't give anything away, do you, Jess?' he murmured.

Her brows rose elegantly. 'I did ask if you wanted cream and sugar.'

He grinned at her evasion. 'I wouldn't have asked *you.*'

'What do you mean?'

'I'd have guessed you'd like it black and strong. No dilutions.'

She might have guessed that about him, too. Cream and sugar weren't his style. 'Am I allowed to smoke now?' she asked.

'It's your home. You don't need my permission.'

'Still, you made your disapproval very clear.' She put down her cup to fetch a cigarette from the small antique dresser against one wall. He didn't offer to light it for her, but sat watching her over the rim of his mug. She took a folder of matches from the narrow drawer, struck one and touched the flame to the tip of the cigarette.

Shaking the match out, she put it on a red Venetian glass ashtray that stood on the dresser, its colour echoing both the border of the carpet and the dominant shade of the large abstract embroidered hanging that graced the wall above.

She leaned back, one hand on the polished satin of the teakwood surface, the other holding the cigarette as she blew a thin trail of smoke into the air through pursed lips. She felt somehow more in control of the

situation than she had sitting in the low chair facing
Gareth across the circle of the equally low table.

'That's a nice piece,' he said, looking at the dresser.
'Where did you get it?'

'An antique shop near the Cross,' she said.

He nodded. At King's Cross, the heart of the city,
one could buy almost anything at any hour of the day or
night, including some rather dubious wares offered
along with the area's raunchy nightlife. He glanced
about the room. 'This place,' he said, 'is . . .
surprising.'

'What did you expect? Art deco? Acres of chrome
and wall-to-wall shag pile?'

'Not exactly. But something more modern and
swept-up, certainly. Not anything as cosy as this.'

'Cosy,' she repeated, grimacing. She looked around
the room critically. 'I'd hoped it was interesting and
comfortable.'

'It is. Also unique, intimate and . . . revealing.'

His eyes caught hers, and she suffered a panicky little
fluttering in her stomach. Unique she didn't mind—it
was a compliment to her taste, she hoped. But intimate
and revealing?

She looked away again, her eyes darting from the
floor to the pictures on the chimney breast, to the
glazed pottery pieces decorating the pelmet shelf over
the window. What did he mean, *intimate?*

He said, 'Aren't you going to drink your coffee? It'll
get cold.'

She picked up the ashtray and walked across to her
chair. Her movements felt jerky and uncoordinated,
totally lacking in her usual sure grace.

Seating herself, she leaned forward to pick up her
coffee. The first few sips steadied her, and she derided

herself inwardly for letting Gareth knock her off balance again. The man enjoyed doing it, it was a deliberate ploy, something he got a kick from, and she wasn't going to allow him to get under her skin.

She took a quick draw on her cigarette and sat back, ostensibly relaxed, blowing perfect smoke rings at the ceiling. One part of her mind was entirely aware of the picture she made: her long legs crossed to one side; the fine fabric of her dress falling softly about her knees and silkily moulding her hips and firm, full breasts; the smooth curve of her throat exposed as she tipped back her sleek head.

'Very clever,' Gareth said drawlingly, as the series of smoke rings ascended towards the ceiling, dissolving shakily on the way. 'Where did you learn to do that?'

'I don't remember. I think Denny taught me.'

'Denny?'

'My husband. Ex.' She lowered her head and let her eyes meet his, testing his reaction.

She couldn't detect any, but there was a longish pause before he said, 'I didn't know you'd been married.'

'Well, now you do,' she said carelessly. 'I live on his alimony. My invisible means of support.'

Something shivered across his face then, just for an instant. Distaste, she thought, and anger flared at his daring to feel that. Denny damned well owed it her, and she had no qualms about his keeping her in relative luxury. Gareth Seymour knew nothing about it. Nothing.

'What about you?' she asked him, the cigarette again lifted briefly to her lips. 'Have you ever been married?'

'No.' He put down his cup carefully on the table. 'Never.'

'My, my!' Her eyes widened in pretended wonder. 'What a cautious, sensible man you are. No smoking, *very* moderate in your alcohol intake, and not even a temporary plunge into the murky waters of matrimony! I didn't know they made them like you anymore.'

'You don't know anything about me, Jess,' he said quietly. 'You've got me taped as stuffy, unfeeling and unimaginative, to say the least, haven't you?'

'Oh, the very least!' she agreed.

'Also cold, hard . . . and cruel. An interesting character assessment on a few fairly brief meetings.'

'That's all right,' she said. 'Anytime. I'll bet you've made a few assessments of me, too, in our short acquaintance.'

He almost smiled, acknowledging it with a slight inclination of his head. 'Right, but I'm not going to tell you. After all, I could be just as wrong about you as you are about me, couldn't I? Now that's an intriguing thought.'

'Is it?' she derided him. 'So how wrong am I about you?'

'Dead wrong.'

It was a temptation to ask him to prove it, but she met his eyes and something stopped her—some premonition of danger, of a risk she had better not take. He was waiting for her to say the words, and if she did he wouldn't hesitate to take her up on them. It was there in his steady gaze, a definite light of warning.

She took refuge in stubbing out her cigarette quite viciously in the ashtray, inwardly castigating herself for cowardice. She looked up again when she was able to face him calmly, a smooth veneer of poise over her ridiculous nervousness. 'More coffee?' she asked him.

'Yes, please.'

She got up and took his cup to the kitchen to refill it. When she came back and handed him the coffee, he caught her wrist as she made to turn away, so that she had to stand still.

'Why don't you sit by me?' he asked her.

'I'm more comfortable over there.'

'Why?'

'The sofa isn't very big.'

'It's quite big enough for the two of us. But if I was planning to leap on you, it wouldn't make a very convenient venue for seduction, if that's what's worrying you.'

Being too close to you worries me! she thought grimly. Having your fingers on my skin like this worries me. There was some crazy chemistry between them that affected her at a touch. The attraction of opposites or something, she supposed. She wasn't sure, though, if it had as powerful an effect on him as it did on her.

She said, 'I didn't suppose for a minute that you were planning to leap on me.'

'Right. So sit down, Jess.' He tugged at her wrist, bringing her closer so that her leg came up against his thigh.

'No!' She pulled away, stepping back, and he held her for just long enough to let her know that she couldn't have escaped him easily if he hadn't allowed her to; then his fingers slackened and fell away.

She sat down in the slipper chair again and looked across at him defiantly, sure that she had won. But when his eyes met hers over the top of the coffee mug there was a glint of satisfaction in them, as though he had just proved something to himself.

He drank his coffee slowly while Jess willed herself

not to fidget, and when at last he put the cup down on the table again she tensed and shifted, ready to stand.

He said, 'Why don't you drive?'

She blinked at the unexpected question. 'I never learned.'

'Why not?'

'I just haven't bothered.'

'Scared?' he suggested softly.

'Of course I'm not scared.'

'I could teach you, if you like,' he offered.

'Thanks,' she said shortly, 'but if I wanted to learn I'd go to a driving school.'

'Pity.'

'Why?' she asked suspiciously.

He smiled. 'Don't you recognise the signs? I'm trying to manufacture an excuse to see you again.'

Something queer happened just below her left breast, as if her heart had shifted position. Weird, she thought, and stupid. She couldn't remember experiencing that sensation since her first adolescent crush.

'Do you need an excuse?' she heard her voice say.

'I'm not sure.' He stood up, and she, too, got to her feet. 'Do I, Jess?'

'Can't you ever just take a chance?' she asked him irritably.

He laughed. 'Maybe I will.'

Without hurry, he came round the little table and reached for her hand, drawing her towards him. She went unresistingly, suddenly overwhelmed by curiosity laced with excitement.

His fingers were warm on her wrist, and the other hand went up to cup her head while he minutely examined her face. His expression was calm, but his eyes held a disturbing glint. She made a slight, protesting movement as though she would pull away, and his hand slipped to her chin, holding it firmly. He tipped her head a little and his mouth descended gently to her cheek; then he made her turn the other way and kissed that cheek, too. Then she felt the butterfly touch of his lips on her forehead, and he stepped back, releasing her chin but retaining his hold on her hand. He lifted her fingers to his lips and kissed each of them, taking his time, then put her palm to his mouth. Fire shot through her as she felt his tongue caress the soft hollow, and then she was free and he was moving away.

'Good night, Jess,' he said quietly. 'I'll see myself out.'

She heard the door close behind him before she was able to move from her trancelike state. She felt stunned, disappointed, fiercely bewildered, vaguely humiliated.

'I need a cigarette,' she mumbled to herself, and went to the sideboard to get one. The hot, acrid taste was soothing, but it made her remember what he had said about tobacco on a woman's breath and wonder if that was why he hadn't kissed her properly. She took the cigarette from her mouth and looked down at it, then made a disgusted, angry little sound in her throat and deliberately took several long, deep pulls at it, drawing the smoke into her lungs. She recalled the feeling of expectancy with which she had felt the touch of his mouth on her cheeks, her temples and her hand, and her savage, unexpected disappointment. She went over to the table and stubbed out the cigarette with hard, furious movements. Crazy, she told herself ruefully in another second. What was she doing? She hollowed her hands in front of her face and blew into them, then sniffed at her own trapped breath. Tobacco, coffee, a hint of the wine that they had been drinking at dinner. What am I doing? she asked herself again. There were plenty of other men who weren't so fastidious about women smoking—and not all of them smoked themselves. Why should she worry?

'I can have any man I want,' she said aloud, addressing the absent Gareth Seymour. It had always been true. She hadn't wanted many, but attracting the attention of those she did had not been a problem. Did she want Gareth? On one level, the most basic, she had to admit the answer was probably yes. But she had learned the hard way that sex was never enough. And what else did they have in common? 'Nothing,' she said aloud. 'Nothing. Absolutely zilch.' Crazy, her mind said again. Crazy to be upset because he hadn't wanted to stay, hadn't even really kissed her, and seemed to find her eminently resistible.

He had hinted strongly that he wanted to see her again, yet not made any real effort to arrange a meeting. Perhaps he had merely been making polite noises, going through the motions expected of a man who had just given a woman dinner. And perhaps something about her had made him change his mind. She hadn't been totally charming, she realised. But then, neither had he.

She had never cared for the man, anyway, she reminded herself. What could it matter to her if he didn't want to see her again, if he was so ultrasensitive that a woman who liked an occasional cigarette and didn't care about speaking her mind was too brazen for him? Nothing, of course. Her restless interior rage was simply a mixture of frustration and hurt pride.

Chapter Three

With Scott and Claire away honeymooning on the island where they had met, Jess felt a surprisingly large hole in her life. She had plenty of friends, but although she deliberately looked up a few of them and arranged several meetings and social engagements, she found herself bored and dissatisfied with their company.

It was ridiculous, she told herself. Scott had always been a restless spirit, travelling often, and Claire was a fairly recent friend with whom she had been on intimate terms for only a very short time. And yet she was aware that with their wedding something inside herself had changed. Or perhaps it had started way back when Scott, with Jess and a group of friends, had landed on the island in the Solomons where Claire was teaching school at the tiny Catholic mission station. It was during their time on Afiuta that Jess had realised she was in danger of falling in love with one of the other men on the trip. Felix possessed a certain rakish sex appeal and knew it all too clearly. He and Jess had sparred and kissed and quarrelled several times before she saw where she was heading and called a halt. On returning to Australia, Jess took a long, hard look at herself and saw that Felix represented a crossroads in her life. He had made no secret of the fact that any relationship between them would be temporary, and she knew that if she succumbed, there would be another short-lived affair after that, perhaps another and another. . . .

She had made enough mistakes with the men in her life. She didn't want to drift from one to the next, guided only by whim and sexual impulse. For a few years after her divorce she thought that was the way to live, lightly and without commitment, skimming over the surface of emotional involvement, disentangling herself when passion threatened to run too deep. It hadn't worked, and with Felix she could see herself being badly hurt when he moved on to some other conquest. It had been hard to turn him down, to bear his piqued anger and lack of understanding. But she had done it, and although it had been surprisingly painful at the time, she felt stronger for it, more able to face life and challenge it head on.

At twenty-eight she felt she had little to show for all those years. A failed marriage, several aborted love affairs, a pregnancy that had miscarried and left her unable to conceive again. Her two brothers had good safe jobs, solid marriages and contented families—not that she ever saw them, but her mother's occasional stiff letters were full of their achievements and virtues and those of their children. Her mother's pride in her sons only underlined her unspoken disappointment in

Jess, her only daughter. Respectable, thrifty and hard-working, the Newalls had been honest, sober people, and from the time Jess entered adolescence she had been a source of worry to them. Bright at school, she had known her teachers thought she should have a university education, but Mr. and Mrs. Newall, holding to the old concept that boys needed higher qualifications more than girls did had pointed out quite gently that their financial position meant that their resources were fully stretched in ensuring that her brothers were sent to university. There was no money to do the same for a girl. Men needed to support their families. In spite of women's lib and what her father termed 'all that nonsense,' girls still got married and left work to raise children. What was a necessity for Bill and Ralph was only an expensive and unaffordable luxury for Jess.

Since hard work would obviously get her nowhere, Jess lost interest in her studies and began to indulge a natural teenage urge to have fun. Being taller than most of her classmates had always made her self-conscious, but at fifteen she was pretty enough to turn heads in the street and some of the boys she had outgrown two years earlier now topped her by several inches. The novelty of being admired and pursued went a long way towards boosting her confidence, and she soon enjoyed the reputation of being a bit of a daredevil, ready for anything.

Her last year at school was largely wasted, although the heinousness of the activities she and her like-minded friends took part in was mostly imagined. But the discovery of a packet of cigarettes in her room, and the fact, defiantly admitted under questioning, that she had secretly attended a party at which drinks flowed freely convinced her parents that she was on a sure path to juvenile delinquency or worse.

Home life became oppressive, with her mother and father monitoring her every move and punishing any infringements of their rigid curfews and regulations with more curtailments of freedom. By turns rebellious and sulky, she gave her well-meaning parents a hard time of it. In later years she was sorry for them, knowing that she had been difficult and unreasonable, but she was never able to get rid of the feeling that they might have tried harder to understand her, nor did she ever quite overcome the resentment she felt towards her brothers. Not only did they receive the education that was denied to her, but their social life was subject to far less restraint, and even smoking and getting pie-eyed on schooners of beer were regarded as natural stepping-stones on their respective paths to manhood. Girls, her father had told her firmly, needed protection; and, according to her mother, ladies didn't smoke, or drink anything stronger than a shandy or a glass of sweet sherry.

When she was able to leave school and get a job in an office, she rejoiced in the financial independence it gave her. When she was earning enough to move into a flat with another girl her mother managed to make her feel thoroughly guilty and ungrateful, and her father predicted huffily that she would be back home within the month.

She managed to keep her first love affair from them, only too happy to avoid taking the man home to meet her family and not realising that his anxiety to 'keep her to himself' masked a strong desire not to be seen with her. The discovery that he was married was shattering, and even more so was the disclosure that his wife was pregnant. She was thankful that her parents, not knowing anything about it, didn't have the opportunity to say 'I told you so.'

After that experience, Denny Wilder had been just what she needed to help her over the bad patch. Undeniably single and frankly uninterested in marriage, Denny had seemed refreshingly honest. He wanted a relationship with no strings, but he adored her body, he said with a suggestive and intentionally funny leer, and could live with the mind that went with it. He was also rich, and Jess wondered afterwards just how much of his attraction for her had been his ability and willingness to buy things they both wanted without counting the cost. The lower-middle-class penny-pinching of her childhood had left its mark and, unadmirable and no doubt immature though it was, she had certainly revelled in the luxury that Denny had provided for her.

Moving in with him had seemed a natural thing to do. She scarcely hesitated when he asked her and, buoyed by his careless brand of love for her and her own excitement at being the object of it, she had hardly given a thought to what her parents would say.

In the event her father had said a lot, and then stopped speaking to her altogether. Her mother had fluttered, cried and thereafter seldom contacted her, her phone calls furtive and reproachful, her letters empty of any real feeling.

Even Jess's marrying Denny hadn't altered her father's view. In his world, marriage came before living together, and certainly before pregnancy, and a shot-gun wedding wasn't much better than no wedding at all.

Jess had got things in the wrong order and he wasn't about to forgive her, ever.

That Denny was so willing to marry her when he realised that he had conceived a child had surprised Jess even more than it had her father. Suddenly protective and enormously thrilled at the idea of parenthood, Denny had been touchingly eager to give the baby his name, and Jess had loved him more in those few months of her pregnancy than ever. It had looked as though her life was coming right at last, and she had even hoped that the reality of having a grandchild might soften her father once the baby actually arrived. She would never know if it might have done. She and Denny were driving home from a party one night, on a wet road, when another vehicle came unexpectedly from an intersection and Denny skidded into a bank and wrecked the car. He was scarcely scratched, but Jess's injuries were more serious and she lost the baby. She kept telling Denny it wasn't his fault, and certainly the other driver had been careless, but in the back of her mind was a niggling suspicion that if Denny had drunk less at the party his reactions would have been faster. She tried not to think about the 'what ifs,' but after the accident it was a long time before she returned to normal.

Too long a time for Denny. While she tried unavailingly to drag herself out of a terrible debilitating depression, he found someone else. Someone who was able to laugh and dance with him, to tease and love him as Jess had before the accident. Denny was made for love and laughter, and Jess was unable to provide it. All that part of her seemed to have been irreparably damaged in the accident and its aftermath. When he asked her for a divorce, she met this new blow with a numbed acceptance that precluded pain. At that time the rift with her family might have been healed. Her mother was prepared to be sympathetic and hinted that her father would come round if Jess made the first move. Stubbornly Jess refused, choking off her mother's clumsy efforts at comfort. If they didn't want her when she was up, she wasn't going to go crawling to them for help when she was down. She had a circle of friends now—Denny's and her friends, and since the divorce was amicable they felt no pressure to take sides. A few of them stood by her while she got through the trauma of the split from Denny and gradually picked up the pieces of her life.

One of those friends had been Scott Carver, and she had reason to be grateful to him. Scott had allowed her to lean on him, been the recipient of some intimate confidences, supported her during more than one bout of despair, and encouraged her first faltering attempts to regain her self-esteem. It had been Scott to whom she had turned when she needed assurance that she was still a whole, attractive, normally functioning woman, knowing that he would understand her compulsion, that he would not despise her for it or misconstrue her motives. And he had not let her down. She didn't know if she could have got through the healing process without him.

Not that she had come through it entirely unscathed. She had learned again to play, to laugh, even to flirt and have a good time, but her tongue had acquired a new waspishness, her manner a superficial carelessness that masked the wariness beneath, concealing her emotions. Scott called it a defence mechanism.

At first Scott had been exempt from her more barbed

comments, until the time when she had tried to repay what he had done for her. Deserted by a woman he had been deeply involved with, he had been going about looking grim for weeks, and Jess had wanted to help, to give back to him some of the loving kindness he had so willingly spent on her. He had accepted her unspoken offer rather cynically and afterwards said, with a gleam of derision in his blue eyes, 'Friends don't have to be repaid, you know.'

Jess had hit him and walked out, furiously angry and not sure why. Who did he think he was—Superman? Were men not supposed to need comforting in distress as women did? *She* was allowed to show weakness, to cry on his shoulder, to look for reassurance from him, but he couldn't take it from her. Men! she thought. Infuriating, impossible creatures.

It was weeks before Scott came to her door, walking in with a faint, rueful smile and kissing her temple as he put his arm about her.

'Sorry, Jess,' he said. 'I guess I was still feeling a bit raw.'

'So you took it out on me,' she said. 'Okay, pal, what are friends for?'

She sounded flippant, but as she made to move from his hold, he tightened his arm, his eyes on her face. Then he bent his head and kissed her lips gently. When he released her she thought his eyes held sadness, but he was smiling. 'Anyway,' he said, fingering his cheek, 'I think the slap had a salutary effect. It cleared my head.'

She gave him her cynical little sideways smile. 'I'm glad.' Critically, she looked at him. 'You look better. Want some coffee?'

'A peace offering?' He reached out a hand to her, and she took it briefly in hers.

'Peace,' she said, smiling. He did look better, less grim and more sure of himself.

'Then, yes, please. I'd like some coffee.'

He knew he had hurt her, and although they remained friends it was not on quite the same footing. She was only rarely able to completely relax her guard with him again. Anyone who knew so much about her, her subconscious warned, had an arsenal of weapons with which to wound, even unintentionally. And Jess had had enough of being hurt.

She found to her dismayed annoyance that she was waiting for Gareth Seymour to contact her again. He didn't, and she decided that he probably had no such intention. She hadn't, after all, given him much encouragement. He wasn't her type, and anyway he was in love with Claire. The last thing she needed was a man who was pining for another woman. Let him find someone else to console himself with.

She was coming out of a second hand book shop at The Rocks one day when she almost bumped into Pietro Benotti. The parcel of books she was holding slipped and he saved it for her. He smiled down at her in a pleased fashion, his eyes roving over her and returning to her face with the frank Italian admiration that he accorded to any pretty woman.

'Claire's young friend!' he exclaimed. 'How delightful to meet you unexpectedly like this, Jess. You are well? But, of course . . . how could you not be when you look so lovely, like a flower just coming into bloom.'

She laughed and thanked him, knowing he was only

paying her what was for him a routine compliment, but it boosted her slightly bruised ego.

'Have you heard from Claire?' she asked.

'A short letter. One does not expect more from a young woman on her honeymoon, you understand,' he said with a gleamingly wicked smile which made her laugh again. 'Please, let me buy you a coffee and I'll tell you all about it.'

There was not much to tell, really, except that Claire seemed ecstatically happy. The islanders had welcomed the honeymooning couple warmly, and Claire was touched at how many of them remembered her and how pleased they were that she had married Scott, whose money and personal interest had helped them to recover from the hurricane which had devastated their villages and crops, and damaged the mission school and hospital, almost a year ago.

'You've been buying books?' Pietro indicated the parcel she had placed on the table as they drank their coffee.

'Secondhand ones,' she told him. 'They're out of print and hard to come by. I was lucky this morning; some of these I've been hoping to get for ages.'

'May I ask what's so special about them?' Pietro asked, intrigued. 'Do you collect rare books?'

'No, not exactly. I like history. I have a few books that might be classed as rare, but I don't collect them for their scarcity value, only for what I can find in them.'

'Then are you studying a particular aspect of history?'

'Well, Australian, mainly. Lately I've been trying to find out more about the women of the convict period. There have been quite a number of books written about the early settlement, but in most of them the place of women was almost ignored. Or given a short chapter somewhere near the end with a lot of tantalising omissions.'

'Omissions?'

Jess made a small grimace. 'Until recently some of the things that went on in the early days were considered unsuitable to be put into cold print.'

'Ah. I see. These days we are less shocked by such things. Are you thinking of writing something on the subject yourself?'

Jess laughed, about to shake her head. Then unexpectedly she felt a sudden twinge of excitement. 'It's an idea. I wonder if I could?'

'Why not? Have you ever done any writing?'

'Not really. I contributed a couple of pieces to my school yearbook, and when I was about eleven or twelve I wrote a few stories and started a novel that I never finished.'

'A novel?' Pietro looked impressed. 'What was it about?'

Jess grinned. 'It was heavily influenced by the Brontës, with a frightfully complicated plot involving the illegitimate son of a British peer, and a deep-dyed villain who wore a black cape and kept the heroine incarcerated in a dark attic.'

Pietro gave her his dazzling smile. 'It sounds exciting. Why did you never finish it?'

'Too lazy, I guess. And . . .' Her face momentarily lost its animation and became closed.

'And?' Pietro prompted gently.

Jess shrugged. 'Well,' she said lightly, 'when I confessed an ambition to be a writer, my brothers hooted with laughter and my parents told me not to be silly. I was going to have to earn a living until I married some nice, suitable boy, and I'd better think of something more sensible. I learned to type, after a fashion, and my mother hoped I'd go into secretarial work, but I was never good enough for that. I became a filing clerk—for a while.'

'And then?'

'Then I got married,' she said abruptly, leaving out the interval in between.

'Ah, yes. Claire told me you had been married. It didn't work out?'

'No. I'm sure Claire will do better.'

'I hope so. Scott is a nice fellow and he loves her. You know him, too, of course?'

'Yes. We're good friends.'

She thought he looked at her rather carefully, and wondered if he was probing to find out just what kind of friendship she had with his son-in-law. She wasn't about to tell him; some things were not to be discussed. She finished her coffee and pushed away the cup.

'Would you do me a favour?' Pietro asked suddenly.

Surprised and a little cautious, she met his eyes and hesitated before asking, 'What?'

'Perhaps you may not want to,' he said, 'but I have to attend a semibusiness function—an evening affair on the twenty-sixth of this month. There will be dancing and supper. I have been asked to make up a party with an acquaintance and his wife, but it's necessary to bring a partner.' He shrugged slightly. 'Since my wife died . . .'

'I'm sure there are any number of women who'd leap at the chance of going with you,' Jess said. He was, after all, a remarkably good-looking man, darkly handsome and with the assurance of maturity.

'Thank you,' he said gravely, a smile lurking in his eyes, 'but you are not one of them, I take it? Of course I'm a little elderly for you. . . .'

'I didn't mean that,' she said swiftly. 'And you're not at all elderly—which I'm sure you know,' she added in dry tones. 'I'd love to go with you, and thank you for asking me.'

'How old are you, Jess?' he asked.

'Twenty-eight. Older than Claire.'

'And a lot younger than me. Please don't worry. I will treat you as . . . perhaps not quite as a daughter'— his black eyes gleamed teasingly—'but as I would wish my daughter to be treated.'

'I'm not at all worried.' She was touched by his anxiety to reassure her, and amused that he felt it necessary. She couldn't remember the last time a man had adopted a protective attitude towards her.

He called for her in a sumptuous Jaguar that he drove himself, and while he complimented her on her appearance she eyed him with appreciation. He might be many years older than herself—probably approaching fifty—but he was still undeniably a very personable escort, and in a ruffled evening shirt and beautifully cut dinner suit he looked extremely distinguished.

The other couple were middle-aged: the man, Joe McNaught, comfortably corpulent, was already perspiring slightly and complaining of the heat; and his wife, Louise, desperately blond and with too much makeup, was wearing a blue synthetic jersey dress that clung closely to a figure any woman might have been proud of. She sparkled visibly under Pietro's murmured compliment and admiring glance as he bowed over her hand, and Jess couldn't help a small grin as she watched. All that automatic Latin charm that he switched on the moment he entered a feminine orbit, and she doubted if he even knew he was doing it!

He came over to her side to escort her to their table, smiling down at her in a questioning way. 'Something amuses you?'

'It's nothing.' Her lips curved again and then set as she stopped short for a moment. Gareth Seymour was sitting at a table adjacent to the one towards which they were headed.

'What is it?' Pietro asked. Then, following her gaze, he said in pleased tones, 'Ah, there is Gareth. You've met him, haven't you?'

'Yes, we've met,' she said as she commenced walking again. She would have liked to sit down immediately, but Pietro excused them both from their hosts and, with his hand on her arm, guided her over to the nearby table to say hello.

Gareth stood up as they approached, shook Pietro's hand and looked appraisingly at Jess as he greeted her smoothly. He introduced them to the woman next to him, Désirée Faulkner, cool and expensive looking, with fine, pale gold hair and exquisite makeup. Jess had seen her with Gareth before. Scott had said she was in the process of divorcing her husband. Perhaps she was a free woman now.

Turning to the older couple at the table, Gareth said, 'And these are my parents.'

Jess's interest sharpened. His father was like Gareth but with hair that had silvered and was receding over a high forehead. His mother was a fading blonde whose aquiline features, elegant bearing and flawless skin proclaimed 'breeding.' She smiled politely at Jess but showed no particular interest. Mr. Seymour's smile was warmer, but, like his son, he gave little away in his expression.

In half a minute Jess and Pietro had returned to their hosts and were sitting at their own table. Jess tried to retain the relaxed mood in which she had begun the evening, but found herself growing increasingly tense. She made an effort to listen to what Pietro, Louise and Joe were saying and managed to make intelligent replies, sipping the drink Pietro got for her and smoking. As she used her lighter for the second time, she caught Gareth's eye on her and experienced a faint, ridiculous sense of guilt before she looked away. Pietro didn't smoke, but Louise puffed jerkily at a cigarette between drinks and Joe lit up a large, strongly scented cigar.

'Have one of mine!' he suggested to Jess with hearty laughter.

She looked at the brown fat sausages and was tempted to accept and blow smoke rings towards the Seymours' table. But she was here as Pietro's guest and she didn't want to embarrass him.

She danced with Pietro, and was pushed around the floor once by a puffing Joe McNaught, averting her eyes from the sight of Gareth leading Désirée Faulkner into the crowd of dancers. As the evening progressed, Joe had become talkative and inclined to laugh a lot. He was nice, she decided, but she preferred dancing with Pietro. His Latin sense of rhythm made him a wonderful mover, and following his lead when he decided to try out some intricate variation was an enjoyable challenge.

Once he smiled down at her and said, 'I feel twenty years younger. I have not enjoyed myself so much for a long time. You're very kind to me, Jess.'

She laughed and said, 'I'm enjoying it, too. And I'm not a kind person. This is sheer self-indulgence.'

'I'm sure that isn't true,' he said, squeezing her hand in his. 'You could never be unkind.'

He was being gallant, and she slanted him a derisive glance but refused to be drawn, even though his eyes sparkled a bold and explicit challenge. After a moment he laughed, hugged her close and then swung her away to indulge in a bit of expert footwork so that it took all her concentration to follow his lead without stumbling. She returned to their table breathless and laughing, and Pietro called for a bottle of champagne.

He was opening it when Gareth came over and asked Jess to dance.

'You don't mind?' he queried Pietro.

'Of course not. We will pour your glass when you have finished your dance with Gareth,' he promised Jess. 'Go on,' he added as she still hesitated.

She couldn't very well refuse. Gareth put his hand lightly on her waist as they walked between the tables to the dance floor, and then brought her smoothly into his arms. In her high heels she was almost as tall as he and their steps matched. Her body curved naturally into his firm hold, and when they turned his thigh brushed against hers. Her eyes flickered and met his, and he smiled at her tautly. Something in his eyes told her that he, too, was conscious of the sexual magnetism between them.

Jess looked away, not wanting to acknowledge it. She felt his hand tighten fractionally. 'Don't stiffen up on me,' he murmured.

'Was I? Sorry.'

'You dance well.'

'So do you.'

'What about Pietro?' he asked.

'He's very good, too. Very Latin.'

'Yes, he has a flamboyant style.'

She glanced up quickly, alert for criticism, but he said, 'You look good together. People have been watching you.'

'I hadn't noticed. We were just enjoying the dancing.'

'What are you doing here with him?'

She looked at him innocently. 'Doing?'

'With Pietro. A bit old for you, isn't he?'

She shrugged. 'So? He's still a very attractive man.'

He glanced over to her table, where Pietro was talking to Louise, whose head was tilted at a coquettish angle as she listened to him. 'Are you attracted to him?' he asked curiously.

'Are you attracted to Désirée?' she challenged him.

A smile tinged his mouth. 'She's thirty-one.'

'And how old are you?'

'Thirty-three.'

'Congratulations,' Jess said sweetly. 'I'd say you're a perfectly matched couple.'

'More than age comes into it.'

'Exactly.'

He looked at her with narrowed eyes for a moment. 'Pietro was very much in love with his wife.'

She wondered what he meant by that but wouldn't ask. Instead she said, 'Then I hope she returned it. He deserves the best.'

'How well do you know him?'

'Well enough,' she parried. 'I'll bet you know Désirée really well.'

'Fairly. What are you so interested in Désirée?'

'Why are you so interested in Pietro?'

'He's a friend—and client—of mine.'

'Oh, so that's why you're asking all these questions?' She looked at him mockingly, daring him to lie. Their eyes met and locked. His mouth curled wryly. The music stopped and for a moment longer he held her. He nodded, a brief, almost infinitesimal inclination of his head, but she knew he wasn't saying yes to her question. It was an acknowledgement that he knew, as she did, what their conversation had really been all about.

Chapter Four

This time she knew that he would contact her. She tried to be cynical about it, sure that it was some primitive male jealousy that had prompted him. Because he had not intended to get in touch again, she was certain, until he had seen her with Pietro.

Dog in the manger, she thought when he phoned. Only that wasn't quite how it was. Because he wanted her all right. Only for some reason he was trying to fight it. She naturally found that rather humiliating. Perhaps it was the cautiousness of the lawyer in him—or perhaps he had some sort of quixotic loyalty to his love for Claire, even though she had chosen someone else.

And perhaps now that he had reluctantly given in to his attraction to Jess he imagined that she would be 'easy'—a palliative for his frustration over Claire.

He had another think coming, she promised herself

mentally as she answered his 'Jess? Are you there?' with 'Yes, where did you think I was?'

'From the sound of the silence, a million miles away, possibly.'

'Does silence have a sound? I was thinking.'

'Does a simple invitation to a show need so much thought?'

'Yes, when it comes from you.'

After a moment's pause, he asked, 'Should I be flattered?'

'I doubt it,' she said dryly. 'I was wondering about your motives.'

'Motives or intentions?' He wasn't telling though, she noticed.

'Both,' she answered promptly.

'Jess?' His voice had lowered to a more intimate, almost teasing note. 'Stop thinking,' he said, 'and say yes.'

The show had received rave reviews. It was full of life and colour and movement, and she enjoyed it, although she was unable to lose herself in it completely, too conscious of the man at her side, of his sleeve brushing her arm, of his thigh close to hers.

A typical Sydney downpour had fallen while they were in the theatre and the pavement was steaming lightly when they came out. He put a hand on her waist, hardly touching her at all, to steer her to his car, but she felt it acutely, as though each fingertip was against her bare skin. He didn't say anything until they were in the car and the engine was running. 'Like to go to a restaurant for a nightcap?' he asked. 'Or a club?'

'No. Too noisy,' she explained.

'My flat then.'

It didn't sound like a question, and she didn't answer. She knew she ought to refuse, to tell him to take her home or to a coffee shop, anywhere else. Instead she turned her head to gaze out of the window, her profile, she hoped, expressing nothing but the purest indifference.

As he drove through streets shiny with rain and colour-washed by city lights, she was glad he didn't talk.

'Come on up,' he said, after garaging the car. His arm about her waist was firmer this time and she stiffened, for a moment refusing to move.

He looked down at her with quizzical surprise. 'Not nervous, are you, Jess?'

'Of you?' She invested the words with delicate contempt, but he didn't seem to take offence, only smiling as though she amused him. 'I just wouldn't want you to take too much for granted,' she said bluntly.

'With you,' he said, 'I take nothing for granted.' His arm left her waist and he took one of her hands in his, swinging it between them. 'Coming?'

She allowed him to lead her into the building. But her warning mechanisms were working overtime, reminding her of her earlier resolve not to be used as second best.

His place was understated, the dominant colours grey and navy. But two large armchairs in powder blue leather flanked a solid mahogany coffee table, and there were thick white sheepskin rugs on the navy blue carpet. A splashy acrylic painting of an outback scene hung on one wall, and books ranging from paperbacks to solid-looking bound volumes filled a bank of shelves on another. Otherwise, Jess decided, the room gave away very little. 'Well?' Gareth said, noting her interest.

'It's like you,' she said.

'No surprises, then?'

He had thought her house surprising, she recalled. Her mouth quirked a little, deriding him. 'No, it's what I expected, more or less.'

'And what was that?'

She shrugged. 'A kind of impersonal good taste, I suppose. Nothing too . . . stimulating.'

His brows rose fractionally. Without comment he smiled, his mouth a little grim. They stood staring at each other, Jess's chin lifting, her gaze daring him to threaten her. The quality of his smile changed. It held genuine enjoyment, and that nettled her, so that her eyes sparked green fire suddenly and she caught her underlip in her teeth, fighting a fierce desire to say something provocative and snarky.

He said softly, 'With a woman like you around, who needs stimulation?'

Before she could get out a suitably caustic reply, he added prosaically, 'The bathroom's off the hallway there, on the right, in case you want to freshen up.'

'I'm fine, thanks,' she told him, and wandered over to look at the books on the shelves.

'Make yourself comfortable,' he said. 'Coffee? Or something stronger?'

'Something alcoholic,' she said, for no other reason than a vague, childish hope that he would disapprove.

He said nothing, but walked to a cabinet that had an antique look about it and brought out a bottle of brandy.

She had taken off her jacket and draped it over one of the chairs, revealing a low-necked, slim-skirted black satin dress, relieved only by a small diamond pendant that swung tantalisingly between her breasts. She was still standing as he turned with two balloon glasses in his hands, and she saw the sudden glitter in his eyes before he veiled them and looked down at the drinks as he carried them over. He had complimented her earlier, in a formal way, on her appearance, but his eyes then had been cool and steady, with the thoughtful look in them that always unsettled her and put her on the defensive.

'Sit down,' he invited, but she took the glass from him first, forcing him to stand near her while she removed it from his fingers, and holding his eyes until she had tasted her drink. She was filled with a jittery excitement but was determined not to let him know it.

Sinking down gracefully on one of the blue chairs, she found that it swivelled and began moving it gently to and fro, just enough to keep her body fluidly in motion. The glow from a standard lamp by the bookshelves played over the black satin sheath in slow waves as she faced him, her legs crossed to one side, the glass in her right hand while the other lay on the arm of the chair.

Sitting opposite, he was holding his drink in the accepted fashion, cradled in both hands to warm it. He would always, she thought, do things the proper way.

His eyes shifted from the amber liquid and went to her left hand. 'Don't you ever wear a ring?'

'A wedding ring? I'm no longer married.'

'I didn't mean a wedding ring. Most women with hands like yours would wear some kind of ring to show them off.'

Jess shrugged. Her gaze strayed to the bookcase, the only real hint of personality about the room unless one counted the painting, and that might have been a decorator's touch. On the top shelf were a Victorian bas-relief vase in blue and white, and a photograph of a fair-haired woman.

For a moment her heart stopped, but it wasn't Claire. She was young and pretty and smiling, but she was not Claire.

She looked at the vase again and then, with renewed interest, over to the cabinet he used for drinks. 'Is that genuine?' she asked him.

'Is it old, you mean? Yes. It's a Georgian wine sideboard.'

'A family heirloom?'

'No.' He lifted his glass and drank some of the brandy.

She said, 'Did you pick it up cheap from someone who didn't know what it was worth?'

He lowered the glass and looked at her, his light eyes expressionless. 'I could afford to pay for it,' he said obliquely.

Knowing she was behaving badly, but driven by a strange, perverse need to keep him at a distance, Jess looked pointedly about the room, her gaze lingering on the plush pile of the carpet, the expensive leather chairs, the finely made table between them that must have cost a pretty penny, and finding for the first time a row of miniatures, hung discreetly near the curtained windows. The miniatures seemed, like the sideboard, to be genuine antiques and were probably almost as valuable.

'Business must be booming in the legal profession,' she said, sipping at her brandy. 'I'm sure you're awfully good at it. I can see you intimidating witnesses with that icy stare of yours.'

'I'm not a criminal lawyer. I deal mostly with companies and contracts.'

'Oh, tax fiddles and that sort of thing. You're obviously a very sharp operator. Done well for yourself, haven't you? Grateful clients?'

He didn't move, but his stillness suddenly lost its relaxed air.

Quite gently, he said, 'If I were a violent man, I'd say you need a lesson in manners.'

She smiled, her mouth sardonic, the slight movement of the swivel chair emphasising her unconcern. 'You relieve my mind,' she mocked him. 'I have nothing to fear from you.'

'I didn't say that.'

She met his eyes and suffered a small but definite shock. Restlessly she got up, placing her glass on the table, and went to the window, suddenly wishing she had a cigarette. She hadn't smoked since lunch, and the strain was beginning to tell.

Her shoulders were grasped from behind. He walked so noiselessly that she hadn't heard him follow her.

He turned her firmly, and she found herself with her back to the wall, his hands holding her and his blue eyes regarding her with detachment. Then he moved closer, pinning her with his body, and she made an involuntary attempt to escape.

He smiled and stopped her, surprising her with his easy, deceptive strength. She realised that struggling would be undignified and possibly futile, and flung her head back to regard him with angry defiance.

'It's what you've been angling for, Jess,' he told her, 'so don't fight it now.'

She flushed with temper, but before she could speak his lips came down on hers, muffling her protest and, without any preliminary persuasion or exploration, drowning her in a sea of sensation.

For seconds she let it happen, let his mouth take hers over, and a quick shaft of desire made her shiver suddenly in his arms. But the anger surfaced again and she closed her mouth, willing her recalcitrant body into resistance. She got her hands between them and pushed at his chest until he raised his head and muttered, 'What's the matter?'

His eyes were bluer than she had ever seen them, hot and brilliant, and his mouth was hardening.

'You've got it wrong,' she said. 'I thought you were too civilised to leap on a woman as soon as you'd lured her into your lair, but I should have known. . . .'

For a moment longer he held her inescapably, and she felt his thighs tense against her own. Then he removed his arms, saying, 'I didn't get it wrong. But I'm not going to force you, Jess. Why are you so defensive with me?'

'Just because I've turned down a pass . . .'

'It wasn't a pass and you know it,' he said curtly. 'But I don't intend to have a postmortem on it. I suppose you want to go home.'

'Please.' She looked at him almost insolently, and he shrugged and picked up her jacket from the chair, holding it out for her.

As she slipped her arms into it, she said unwillingly, with a lightness that didn't quite come off, 'It isn't only you. I'm defensive with everyone. Ask Scott.'

She still had her back to him when he said, 'Does Scott know so much about you?'

'Probably more than anyone.' She turned. For a moment their eyes clashed; then he put his hand on her arm and took her to the door.

'I can get a taxi,' she offered, her voice brittle.

'Don't be silly,' he answered patiently. 'I'm not the kind of man who sends his date home in a taxi because she doesn't want to stay the night.'

'Always the gentleman!' she jeered.

'Yes, aren't I?' His eyes warned her suddenly not to push him too far, and to her secret chagrin she yielded, accompanying him silently to the car and getting in meekly when he opened the door for her.

On the way she said abruptly, 'I don't suppose you'd have a cigarette in the glove box?'

'No. Sorry.'

'Are you?' she asked wryly.

'I'll stop and get you some if you like,' he said.

'Never mind. I guess you wouldn't like me to smoke in the hallowed precincts of your vehicle, anyway.'

'Stop it, Jess,' he said, almost wearily.

He sounded like a father with a recalcitrant child. Irritated, she said, 'It's the strain—of being without a cigarette.'

'Did you forget to bring them?'

'No,' she said with exasperation. 'I left them behind deliberately because I know you don't like them.'

'Thank you,' he said gravely, 'for being so considerate.'

She looked at him, suspecting sarcasm, but when he glanced at her she didn't see any. 'The first thing I'm going to do when I get home,' she said tartly, 'is light one up.'

He laughed quietly, his eyes on the road ahead. 'Just as you like.'

Well, why should he care, she thought, unreasonably aggravated. It was his own comfort and health he was thinking of, not hers.

But at least he had really kissed her tonight.

She pushed the thought away. Kisses were two a penny. She had only responded as she had because . . . oh, because it was a long time since she had been kissed. And because of whatever it was that created that odd spark between the two of them. But she could see no future in a relationship with Gareth Seymour. And she was too old and too jaded for any more temporary relationships.

When he had left .her at the door, she closed it carefully behind him and made for the kitchen. Coffee and a cigarette, she promised herself. Something to soothe her jumping nerves. She had half thought that he might kiss her again, but he hadn't touched her, so there was no reason for her taut restlessness except that he seemed to affect her that way.

She made a cup of coffee, went through into the little sitting room and, flipping the lid of the cigarette box, picked one out. With it and a folder of matches in her hand she sat on the slipper chair and tasted the coffee before putting the cup down to light the cigarette.

The first luxurious, long-anticipated drag should have been balm. The smoke curled into her lungs and the tobacco taste lingered on her tongue pungently, strangely unpleasant.

It was the long break, she thought confusedly, since the last one. Only since lunch? Hours—how many hours? More waking hours than she'd spent without smoking for years, anyway. Unbelievably, enough to spoil the taste. She took the cigarette from her lips and regarded it, the white, thin paper, the pale gold filter tip. Her usual brand. Something wrong with the tobacco? No. Only that this was almost like tasting it for the first time.

A few puffs and she'd be enjoying it. It wasn't that easy to give up. She lifted it again to her lips, touched them with the filtertip and lowered it again. Give up? She'd done it once, hadn't she? On impulse she leaned over and stubbed the thing out decisively in the ashtray.

On her way to bed she passed the box on the sideboard again and stretched out her hand, hesitated, then quickly took out one of the tempting white cylinders. The matches lay beside the box. She placed the unlit cigarette in her mouth and stood staring at the small square folder. She never smoked in bed. Never.

She picked up the box and carried it into the bathroom and emptied its contents down the toilet, removed the cigarette from her mouth and added that, too. Fetching her handbag from her bedroom she found the new pack in there, quickly tore it open and flushed the lot away, grimacing at the strong smell of wet tobacco that lingered afterwards. Then she sat on the edge of the bathtub and put her hands to her forehead and told herself that she was mad, quite mad. She fiercely wanted a cigarette, but she hadn't left one in the house.

She was asked to attend another wedding. They seemed to be in season, she reflected without pleasure as she pushed the silver-edged card back into its envelope. This one specified 'and partner,' and she was tempted not to go. But curiosity warred with disinclination. Sheryl Marsh and Morris Quinn had both been on Scott's yacht, along with Jess and another couple, brother and sister, when they had landed on Afiuta and met Claire. Sheryl, Jess thought, had been out of her depth in more ways than one. She suspected that the girl was from a less moneyed background than any of the others except for Jess herself. Her clothes were good and she seemed to have jewellery galore, but she wore them with a self-consciousness that betrayed her. She name-dropped a lot and behaved at times with a studied snobbery that grated. Reluctantly Jess had been sorry for her, especially since she had come on the cruise with Felix, who had made no effort when he became bored with her to hide the fact, blatantly turning his roving eye on Jess.

Possibly, Jess thought, the invitation was some kind of attempt to 'show' her that Sheryl had still come out on top. Morris had money, and if he was hardly every girl's dream as far as looks went, he wasn't actually repulsive. Sheryl was the kind of girl to whom marrying money would be a life's ambition realised.

People in glass houses, Jess chided herself harshly. She had married a wealthy man and still used Denny's money without compunction to live on. And what was the use of telling herself that that was different? Didn't everyone think their own sordid little reasons for doing less than noble things were unique and acceptable? Sheryl had seemed to have no family and few friends. Perhaps she just wanted a respectable showing of 'the bride's friends' to support her on her big day.

Still, Jess couldn't see herself attending without a personable partner. Gareth sprang immediately to mind, but she wasn't going to give him an opportunity to rebuff her, or more grounds for thinking she was 'angling' for his kisses. Reviewing her male acquaintances, she rejected one after the other on various grounds until she thought of Pietro Benotti. He was impressive enough to ensure that no one could think she was incapable of snaring as good a catch as Morris Quinn or that she had been unable to hold Felix after all.

Pietro declared himself delighted to return the favour she had done for him and partner her to her friend's wedding. Perhaps prompted partly by conscience, Jess dispatched an extravagant present, a set of silver tableware in an elaborate design that she hoped would satisfy Sheryl's taste for ostentation.

The wedding was very traditional: the bride wearing a spectacular concoction of white lace and satin, the groom almost handsome in morning clothes; the speeches at the reception interminable. An uncle had given Sheryl away, and one of the bridesmaids was some sort of cousin. So she did have some family, if not parents, after all. Surprisingly, Pietro seemed to enjoy himself. Catching his mood, Jess managed to wring some pleasure from the occasion, too. Looking at the presents that were displayed in the reception rooms, they saw that Scott and Claire had sent a large boxed set of matching satin sheets and pillowcases.

'When are they returning from their honeymoon?' Jess asked. 'Claire said a couple of months. . . .'

'Next week. They have stretched it to nine, nearly ten weeks. Well, Scott is lucky, he has very competent people to run his business. By the way, I want to give a small party to welcome them home. You must come.'

Sheryl, flushed and smiling and very bridal, swept up to them, her eyes resting with curiosity on Pietro. Turning to Jess, she said, 'Oh, you're looking at Scott and Claire's present. Lovely, isn't it? And I loved the silver, Jess. It must have cost you an awful lot.'

Inwardly wincing, Jess smiled. 'Not really. I'm glad

you like it. Have you met Pietro Benotti? He's Claire's stepfather.'

'*Really?*' Sheryl's voice went squeaky with excitement. 'I had no *idea!* He's with *you?*'

Pietro answered, his lips twitching. 'That's right, I am with Jess. Allow me, please, to offer my best wishes to you, Mrs. Quinn, and I must tell you what a beautiful bride you are. Your husband is most fortunate, the envy of every man here.'

Blushing, Sheryl fluttered her lashes at him. 'Oh, thank you! I'll tell you what, if I wasn't a married woman I'd be envying Jess.'

Pietro roared with laughter and kissed her hand gallantly.

'Mind you,' Sheryl said, looking at Jess with winsome candour, 'it wouldn't be the first time. On that trip we took together all the men were smitten with Jess.'

'Nonsense!' Jess protested.

'Maybe not Morris,' Sheryl conceded with sweet smugness, 'but Felix certainly was, and I'll bet Doug tried to make it with you. . . .'

'Doug would have tried it with anyone. I'll bet he did with you, too.'

Ignoring that, Sheryl went on, 'And I always thought there was something between you and Scott.'

'Then you were wrong!' Jess said crisply.

Sheryl opened her mouth, blushed again and glanced at Pietro, muttering, 'Oh, sorry. I forgot . . . about Claire. Well, I guess I was mistaken, then,' she said unconvincingly.

When she had gone back to Morris's side, Jess could feel Pietro's thoughtful regard on her. Crossly she said, 'Sheryl's as silly as they come.'

'A pretty little chatterbox,' Pietro agreed blandly. 'Does she have any reason not to really like you, Jess?'

'No . . . Oh, perhaps she does,' Jess amended honestly. 'But it really wasn't my fault.'

'A beautiful woman cannot help her beauty.' His hand on her shoulder was kind, but the thoughtful look in his eyes had not entirely receded.

Pietro's party to welcome the honeymooners home was held on the Saturday after their arrival. Jess had known that Gareth would probably be invited, but his phone call was unexpected.

'Pietro tells me you're going to his party. Could I call for you?'

'Did he ask you to pick me up?' she demanded.

'I didn't need to be asked. I know you don't drive and as we're both going . . .'

'All right,' she said. 'Thanks for the offer.'

She still had a sneaking suspicion that it had been Pietro's idea. Remembering that long, pensive look he had given her after Sheryl's artless witterings, she wondered if he was taking care of his step-daughter's interests by making sure that Jess had an escort.

She had bought a new dress, a discreet creamy beige georgette, adding a gold chain belt and necklace, amber drop earrings and a narrow matching bangle worn with two gold ones. She was ready early, but left her jacket and purse lying on the bed so that she wouldn't look eager, and spent ten minutes prowling about her sitting room and wishing for a cigarette. When Gareth came she asked him in while she fetched her things from the bedroom and unnecessarily checked her appearance in the mirror, fiddling with her hair and wondering if it was time she had it cut.

Flinging the jacket carelessly about her shoulders, she picked up the bag and went to join Gareth, a social smile pasted on her face.

She had left a pile of books, from which she had made some notes, on the coffee table, and he was sitting on the sofa leafing through one of them, a facsimile edition of a First Fleet journal kept by one of the sailors.

Glancing up at her, he said, 'I haven't come across this before.'

'We've plenty of time. Finish it.'

He shook his head. 'I'd want to read it properly.' Returning to the open page, he smiled and read out, ' "Heavy weather. Pumping ship. A report that convicts have struck their irons and 'threted' to take the ship proved false. Captain ordered extra rum for sailors pumping to 'squench' their thirst." Almost like being there, isn't it?'

'Borrow it if you like,' Jess said. 'It isn't an original.'

He smiled with genuine pleasure. 'Thank you. If you're interested in originals, I could show you some. My people have a small library of old journals, diaries and records.'

She couldn't hide the excitement in her eyes. But she hesitated about answering him.

'Well?' he prompted. 'You're obviously an avid reader of history'—he glanced at the books on the table, all of them concerned with Sydney's early days— 'although when I asked you once before if it interested you I got fobbed off.'

Not acknowledging the implied reproof, she admitted, 'I'd like to see them, if it's not too much trouble.'

'No trouble. We'll make a day, and I'll take you to Karunja and you can browse through what we have.'

'Karunja?'

'My family home.'

'A nineteenth-century mansion, no doubt,' she said resignedly. 'I knew your family must be First Fleeters. And officers and gentlemen, I'll bet.'

'Officers, yes.' He paused. 'As for the other, I don't think there were too many gentlemen among the soldiers in the early colony, even the higher-ranking ones. A good number of them seem to have been greater rogues than the convicts they were guarding.'

'I know, but not *your* ancestors, surely?' She gave him a look of feigned shock.

'We'd all like to believe that our own forbears were the exceptions.' He stood up, holding the journal in one hand. 'I promise to return this in good order. Shall we go?'

The party turned out to be a buffet dinner for about thirty people. Both Claire and Scott looked tanned and happy, and kept exchanging intimate glances and quick smiles.

Pietro beamed on them with fatherly pride and dropped occasional teasing remarks into the conversation, which Scott parried with lazy good nature. Then he mentioned Sheryl's wedding, and Claire said with surprise, 'You were there?'

'With Jess,' Pietro explained. 'We had a delightful day.'

Jess wasn't looking at Gareth, seated beside her, but she felt the sudden intensity of his stare. Later, when they were in a corner of the lounge, drinking some of

Pietro's excellent wine, Gareth said, 'You've been seeing quite a lot of Pietro, then?'

Twice wasn't a lot. 'I needed a partner for the wedding,' she said.

'You could have asked me.'

She stared at him deliberately, her green gaze satirical. 'So I could.'

His eyes hardened. 'Or any of a dozen others, I suppose.'

Shrugging, she said nothing. He could suppose whatever he liked. 'They seem happy,' she said, casting about for a change of subject. 'Scott and Claire, I mean.'

'Are you disappointed?'

She stared at him frostily. 'Certainly not. Are you?'

'I'm not the one who professed to be a cynic,' he reminded her. His eyes finding the guests of honour, he said, 'Do you think Claire might have put on a little weight?'

'It wouldn't hurt. She's always been slim,' Jess observed truthfully. Her own more voluptuous figure seemed overlush compared with Claire's daintier curves. Looking at her friend now, she thought that Gareth could be right, though.

Gareth shifted his attention from Claire and finished the drink in his hand. Jess sipped hers and sat playing with the bracelets on her arm. They jangled slightly and she stopped as Gareth glanced over at them, his gaze lingering.

Someone nearby was smoking, and she moved restlessly in her chair, taking a gulp of wine that left her glass empty.

'More?' he asked her politely.

Jess shook her head, regarding the pink dregs gloomily and wishing the smoker would move away. She didn't think she could stand it much longer. 'Can we get some fresh air?' she finally asked with quiet desperation.

'Of course.' Gareth got up at once and led her onto the same small balcony he had found for her the day Scott and Claire were married. *Déja vu*, she thought, embarrassed by the memory. It was black night this time and the harbour was invisible except for reflected lights trailing shimmering ribbons of colour into the water.

'If you want a cigarette,' Gareth said, 'don't mind me.'

'I don't want one!' she said, lying in her teeth. 'Do you think I can't live without them?'

A slight pause ensued. '*Can* you?'

He sounded mildly amused, and she snapped back, 'Yes! I haven't had one in weeks, if you want to know!'

'Congratulations. Is that why you're in such a foul mood?'

'I am *not* . . .' she rounded on him, then stopped, biting her lip, and turned away again. 'Sorry,' she muttered.

'Hard, isn't it?'

'How would *you* know?'

'I've been through it with several of my friends. Ex-smokers are a bit like religious converts—eager to share their experiences with anyone who'll listen.'

'Well, don't worry. I don't intend to bore you with my withdrawal symptoms,' she promised him, her voice tart.

He caught her hand in his, bringing her towards him.

His expression in the darkness was unreadable. 'One thing you never are, Jess,' he said, 'is boring.'

He framed her face with his fingers and kissed her lingeringly, his mouth warm and firm. Jess clutched at the metal railing behind her, but that didn't stop her mouth from returning the kiss.

He raised his head and impatiently brought his hands to her waist, pulling her away from the railing, and as he kissed her again her arms went up to embrace him.

When he released her she turned blindly back to the rail, holding it until the metal bit into her palms, and breathing slowly and carefully.

'Are you all right?' he asked her, his voice oddly muffled.

Jess managed a little laugh. 'Of course. I've been kissed before—and by experts.'

'I don't doubt it. I'm not a novice myself.'

'I noticed,' she said on a breath.

'Well, at least it took your mind off your other craving for a while.'

'I'll recommend you as a therapist if you like,' she offered.

'Thanks, but I think one . . . client . . . is as much as I can handle right now.'

As they reentered the big lounge Claire came up to them and said, 'You must both have dinner with us soon. Can we make a date now?'

Trapped, Jess agreed with a semblance of enthusiasm. She wasn't sure if Claire was treating them as an entity or doing a bit of blatant matchmaking. Either way she didn't see any graceful way to wriggle out of it and neither, apparently, did Gareth. When Claire had left them she turned to look at him, trying to gauge his reaction. He merely raised his brows a fraction and looked blandly back at her. There was no way of knowing what he thought.

He went to replenish their drinks, and Pietro strolled over to Jess. 'You and Gareth are enjoying yourselves?' His smile was bland, his eyes filled with lively curiosity. He had noticed their absence while they were on the balcony, of course.

'Yes,' she said, daring him to comment.

He laughed and gracefully changed the subject. 'Have you thought any more about writing a book, Jess?'

'Yes, actually. In fact, I've even done some preliminary research and roughed out a story.'

'Splendid. I will look forward to seeing it published.'

Jess laughed. 'That's a long way off.' Seeing Gareth returning, she said hastily, 'I haven't even mentioned it to anyone else. I don't want to talk about it yet.'

He glanced round and nodded his understanding. When Gareth joined them Pietro was talking about something altogether different. But Jess noticed the keen glance that Gareth gave them both before handing her a glass.

His good-night kiss at her door was restrained, although he still managed to make her tingle all over, and he didn't ask to stay. She wondered if he was feeling trapped, too. He had, after all, been a bachelor for a long time. If Pietro and Claire were matchmaking, their plans were definitely for matrimony and nothing less. They had perhaps been less than subtle, and Gareth wasn't a man to be manipulated.

Chapter Five

On Monday Jess bought a typewriter.

It was years since she had attempted to type, and at school she had never been good at it, but with the help of the simple instruction book that had come with the portable electric machine, she found that the rudiments of touch-typing were reasonably simple to master—in theory. In practice she produced whole lines of typed nonsense from placing her hands wrongly on the keys, and rows of identical letters when she accidentally depressed one for too long.

Eventually she decided that the only way was to start again from scratch with the boring, repetitive exercises prescribed in the book. At first the novelty helped, but by Wednesday evening she was ready to scream with frustration, yet all the more determined to master this apparently simple skill if it killed her.

The knock on the door broke her concentration, and she swore under her breath as she went to answer it.

Gareth said, 'I brought your book back. Am I disturbing you?'

She hadn't been getting very far, anyway. 'Come in,' she said resignedly, taking the journal from him. 'Did you enjoy it?'

'Very much. The routine bits are so unexpectedly relieved by delightful surprises. You get pages of entries on the weather and complaints about the food, and then suddenly there's a threatened mutiny or the cook goes mad or the first mate is found in his bunk with a beautiful stowaway—'

Jess objected, 'The journal didn't say she was beautiful.'

He smiled. 'Wishful thinking. And I daresay any female would have looked pretty good to men who'd been at sea for several months.'

He caught sight of the typewriter that she had put on a small table in the corner of the sitting room, and said, 'I didn't know you were a typist.'

'I'm not,' she said shortly. 'I doubt that I ever will be. I've just been practicing.'

He walked over and looked at the paper in the machine.

Amused, he glanced at her and said, 'Stick with it. Why do you want to learn?'

Carelessly she said, 'It's something to do. I thought it might be fun.'

'Job skills never come amiss.'

'I don't need job skills,' she told him. 'Unless my ex-husband's money runs out.'

His face went woodenly expressionless. Well, it was what she had expected. 'You don't approve of me, do you?' she asked him.

'I don't disapprove of you,' he said. 'I just think . . .'

'Well, don't stop there. Go on.'

'You're determined to start a quarrel, aren't you?'

'Of course not. I'm curious about your opinion of me.'

'Does my opinion matter?'

The question startled her and, unexpectedly, swift color flared in her cheeks. 'Not specially,' she told him quickly. 'I'm just interested.'

'Really?' He drawled the word. 'Well, since you want to hear it, I'll tell you what I think. I think you're a fool. You're young and healthy, intelligent and energetic, and you're frittering away your time playing at life, finding toys'—he waved a hand at the typewriter—'to occupy your time when your social life gets slack.'

'Well, what am I supposed to do then? Become one of the world's workers? Haven't you heard there's an unemployment problem? Do I take a job from some poor man with six children or some woman with babies and a mortgage and a husband in a lower-income bracket?'

'You've enough brains, surely, to find something worthwhile to do that wouldn't take bread from someone else's mouth . . . if it's your conscience that bothers you.'

With a glittering smile, she said, 'You're right, of course, it isn't my conscience. So don't think you can persuade me to start doing meals-on-wheels or something. That's not my style.'

'What is your style, Jess?'

Her mouth twisted wryly. 'Quite different from your Protestant work ethic, I'm afraid. My parents were two of the world's workers and all it got them was a narrow, miserable little life of respectable dreariness. I *like* being one of the idle rich. Don't try to change me.'

'It just surprises me that a woman with your kind of aggressive pride is willing to live off someone else for the rest of her life.'

'You don't know anything about it. How dare you stand there judging me . . .!'

'I'm not judging!' He had raised his voice slightly. 'Whatever I've said, you asked for it.'

She had, too. And got more than she bargained for. 'You don't pull your punches, do you?' she said. 'You really ought to do criminal work. You'd be devastating in a courtroom. They'd make you a Queen's Counsel in no time. You'd probably end up on the Bench, with a knighthood.'

'Why do I keep feeling we've had this conversation before?' he asked with sarcasm. Then he added more soberly, 'I'm sorry if I hurt you.'

She gave him a brittle smile. 'Don't be silly! I'm indestructible. I've forgotten what it's like to be hurt.'

'If I thought that was true I'd be very sorry for you.'

'You disappoint me. You mean under that hard surface there's a heart as soft as butter? I don't believe it.'

He shook his head, smiling slightly. 'You needn't be afraid of hurting me, Jess,' he said.

She stared at him and said flippantly, 'That makes two of us, then. Can I get you a drink?'

She thought he was going to refuse, but he said, 'Yes, thanks. Whisky, if you have it.'

She poured one for herself, too, and they sat opposite each other, warily, until he laughed and said, 'We always seem to get off on the wrong foot, somehow, don't we? I wonder why?'

Suddenly tired of skirting round it, Jess looked at him directly. 'You know why.'

The surprise in his eyes was quickly succeeded by reluctant acknowledgement. 'You're very blunt,' he said. 'So . . . what are we going to do about it?'

'Nothing,' she said calmly, and took a sip from her glass. 'Not a damn thing.'

'You're so sure.' The spark in his eyes might be anger or chagrin—or a bit of both, she supposed.

'I don't need sex for the sake of it,' she told him. 'And you've never really thought much of me as a person, have you?' Without waiting for him to answer that, she went on cruelly, 'Anyway, I don't think I even like you at all.''

His jaw went tight, his eyes narrowing for a moment. 'Thanks,' he said. 'Those are pretty sweeping statements.'

She shrugged. 'Just honest.'

He finished his drink and stood up. 'Well, it seems I've outstayed my welcome. Do I collect you on Friday evening?'

'What?'

'Dinner,' he reminded her, 'with Claire and Scott. We're both invited, remember?'

'Of course I remember. All right, then . . . if you want to.'

He looked at her thoughtfully, his lips slightly pursed. 'Oddly enough, I think I do.'

The Carvers' home was no mansion, but from Darling Point it commanded a high-priced view of the harbour and the city skyline. The well-established garden boasted a variety of flowers, including a whole bed of banksias, the long flower cylinders ranging from green through pure yellow to amber and an almost rust-colored brick red. A wide-spreading jacaranda was in full, fernlike leaf, the remains of purple blossoms still staining the grass at its feet, and a tall cabbage tree with pom-poms of spiky leaves towered above one corner of the red tiled roof. Jess smiled as they reached the door and rang, thinking that Scott was indulging Claire's need for permanence, and wondering if his wandering ways would be curbed by his love for her. The quiet, suburban atmosphere was rather different from Scott's former life-style, racing custom-built cars, sailing his own yacht round the Pacific, exploring remote corners of New Guinea. . . .

The door opened, and she saw Gareth's eyes soften as he bent to kiss Claire's cheek.

The two women hugged each other with affection, and as Claire closed the door Scott came into the small lobby. Jess went to him, holding out her hands to be taken in his, and they kissed lightly. He slipped an arm about her waist as the other two came toward them, and held out his right hand to Gareth.

As Gareth took it, Jess saw the tender expression that he had worn for Claire replaced by a curiously assessing look. Not for the first time, seeing them together, Jess was struck by the contrast between the two men. Scott was taller and broader, strikingly good looking with his sun-streaked hair and vivid blue eyes, but Gareth's leaner features had a less obvious distinction and his lighter eyes a penetrating quality that made them strangely arresting. And she knew what unexpected physical strength his lithe body possessed.

Scott, too, behind the social smile that he wore, was regarding his guest with a look of appraisal, sizing him up. Their hands gripped for a few long seconds while they exchanged conventional greetings, and Jess was aware of a certain tension in the air, a mutual guardedness between them.

Then Claire was ushering them into the lounge, Scott's hand leaving Jess's waist as she went before him to sit in a comfortable, tweed-covered armchair. There were four chairs grouped in front of a bay window overlooking the water; an inviting arrangement suggesting interesting conversation, with a tranquil view to rest the eyes.

The room had a quiet, understated elegance that combined Claire's taste and Scott's money. Claire's fair prettiness had become true, glowing beauty, and she had acquired a new poise and confidence in the certainty and security of her husband's love. Jess had guessed some time ago that Claire, virtually abandoned by her mother when she was placed in a convent orphanage at eight years old, had a dire need to know that someone loved and cherished her above all others.

'What shall we drink to?' Scott asked when they each had a glass in their hands.

'The future?' Claire suggested.

Scott gave her a warm, private smile and put out his hand to cover hers where it lay on the arm of her chair.

'The future,' he said softly, and raised his glass first to her and then to the others.

Jess echoed the toast, and Gareth silently concurred. She saw his eyes resting on Scott's and Claire's joined hands.

Claire took only a sip and sat holding her glass while they talked, until she put it down on the table to go and check the dinner.

'Can I help?' Jess asked.

'No, thanks, everything's almost done. It's just a matter of dishing up, really.'

Jess sat back in her chair, oddly relieved that the two men would not be left alone. She had what she told herself was an irrational feeling that it wouldn't be safe, although they were talking quite amicably. Still, she was uneasy, and when Claire called them to the table she was the first to stand up.

By the time Claire served a sweet of fruit and cream some of the tension seemed to have dissolved, and Jess, at least, felt much more relaxed. The conversation had ranged from politics to the needs of the less affluent Pacific island communities to corporate business practice and, on a more personal level, the Carvers' recent honeymoon and their plans for the future.

'Are you settling down at last?' Jess teased Scott. 'Or is Claire going to be carted half way round the world on some yachting adventure?'

'Not at the moment, anyway.' He smiled. 'Claire has to be looked after.' His smile slanted to his wife and she flushed, laughing at him.

'You might as well tell them,' she said. 'I can see that you're dying to.'

Scott looked strangely abashed. 'Okay. Claire's

pregnant,' he announced, grinning like a proud boy. 'We're going to have a baby.'

For a moment Jess was stabbed by a shaft of pure envy. She looked away quickly, fighting it, and found her eyes meeting Gareth's hard, knowing stare. Then she took a deep breath and said quickly, with utter sincerity, 'That's wonderful news. I'm so glad—for both of you. When?'

'June,' Claire said, looking slightly embarrassed. Jess wasn't the counting kind, but from Claire's comical expression she could only guess that it had happened fairly shortly after the wedding.

Gareth added his congratulations and proposed another toast. On their way home afterwards he said, 'You've been very quiet since dinner.' Deliberately he added, 'Weren't you pleased with their news?'

'Of course I'm pleased,' she said. 'It seems awfully soon, though.'

'Yes,' he agreed. 'I suppose, with Claire being as strongly Catholic as she is, she wouldn't have wanted to try and prevent it.' He paused. 'You're not suggesting . . .?'

'Of course not,' she scorned. 'Claire is definitely not that sort of girl.'

'No, she isn't.'

'You'd know, of course.'

'For the record,' he said with mild emphasis, 'I didn't even try. So in the sense that you mean, no, I wouldn't know.'

'Was it her air of virginal purity?' Jess asked. 'Or the fact that Pietro would have had your head on a platter?'

'Neither.' He glanced at her. 'I thought you were a friend of hers.'

'I am.' In the darkness, she flushed. 'I'm extremely fond of Claire, and I wasn't being insulting.'

'Weren't you?' He sounded sceptical.

Smarting, she thought, let him think me a cat if he wants to. She didn't suppose that his opinion of her could sink much lower than it already was. When he stopped outside the house she was unprepared for his hand on her arm preventing her from getting out of the car and drawing her firmly against him. The kiss, when it came, was almost angry in its intensity, an expression of some built-up frustration, and for a moment her whole being rejected it. But her resistance melted under the force of his desire, and her own. . . .

When his mouth left hers she gave a sobbing sigh and tried to move out of his arms, but he merely turned her deftly so that she was lying across his lap, her head tipped against his shoulder, and then he was kissing her again, long and deep, his hand shaping the contours of her breast, waist, thigh, slipping smoothly under her skirt. . . .

'No!' She wrenched her mouth away from its passionate imprisonment and began to struggle.

He let her sit up but held her shoulders. His thigh pressed warmly along the length of hers. 'Jess . . .'

'No!' she repeated.

He took her head into his hands and made her give him her mouth again, compelling her acquiescence if not her response. And this time, with an effort of will, she managed to withhold it.

When he realised that her determined rigidity was not going to weaken, he lifted his mouth at last and, with his lips on the soft skin of her throat, groaned a single word, 'Why?'

She said, her voice hoarse with strain, 'I won't be a substitute for Claire—or anyone else.'

He was very still. 'Substitute?' He drew back, staring down at her, his face blurred in the dim light. 'As if you could be anything of the sort!' he said harshly. 'You're nothing like her.'

She had told him that he couldn't hurt her, but it wasn't true. Flinching inwardly, she taunted him in self-defence, 'Didn't she ever kiss you back?'

He was silent for a long moment. His hands had returned to her shoulders and she felt his fingers tighten on her flesh. In a strange tone he said, 'Yes, she did, as a matter of fact. But not in the way you do.' Then, his voice hardening, he said deliberately, 'What about you, Jess? Was that me you were kissing just now, or Scott?'

About to say *You're crazy!* she closed off the words abruptly, afraid of giving herself away. 'Let's call it a night, shall we?' she suggested. 'I've had about enough.'

He said harshly, 'Supposing *I* haven't?'

'Tough luck,' she returned. 'Let go of my shoulders, will you!'

He was tempted to refuse and she knew it. They glared at each other, faces shadowed, eyes gleaming with anger. Then he slowly sat back, releasing her. 'You'll excuse me,' he said coldly, 'if I don't see you to the door?'

He waited until she got there, though, before he started the car and drove off into the night.

She was almost asleep when the telephone rang. 'Jess,' he said, 'I'm sorry. And, Jess—you're not a substitute. Never.'

She was silent with surprise, trying to think of words to answer him, but after a second or two she heard the click in her ear as he hung up.

He phoned again in the morning, late. 'If you're free,' he said, 'we could go to Karunja this afternoon and I'll show you our library.'

'Yes,' she said, 'I'm free. Thank you.'

Karunja was a Jacobean-style sandstone mansion overlooking the Lane Cove River that flowed into the Parramatta. Jess was unsurprised to find it furnished largely with antiques, and chandeliers dripping from the high ceilings. Determined to be on her best behaviour, she had confined the conversation in the car to harmless chitchat, and when Gareth's mother offered a ladylike hand to her on their arrival, she smiled nicely as she took it in her own firm grasp.

'It's kind of you to let me see your library,' she said, feeling like Eliza Doolittle.

'Not at all. Gareth says you're interested in history.' Her hostess sounded mildly surprised. 'You'll join us for afternoon tea when you've seen the collection?'

'Thank you.' Mrs. Seymour made her feel like someone who was there on business rather than a guest, but perhaps that was just her manner.

Gareth said, 'I'd like to show Jess over the house first, if that's all right, Mother.'

'Yes, of course. Your father's away golfing, but he said he'd be back by four.'

'Right, we'll see you later then.' He took Jess's arm.

'Are you a golfer, too?' she asked him as he steered her towards the back of the house.

'No, tennis is my game and in the winter I play a bit of squash.'

That explained his physical fitness in spite of his sedentary indoor work, she supposed.

They entered a vast kitchen that harboured an enormous old black iron stove. 'Not used anymore, of course,' Gareth said. The former scullery had been turned into a modern kitchen with an electric stove, an island table, and a U-shaped bench round three walls holding a food processor, electric toaster, electric fry-pan and stockpot. 'All mod cons, in fact,' Jess said.

'Yes. My mother's very happy here.'

'She does the cooking herself?'

'Mostly. When they entertain she often has help.'

The entertaining was done in the English oak panelled dining room, which he took her to next, with its long polished table and carved chairs beautifully preserved from the previous century. He showed her a huge drawing room that looked like a museum, admitting, 'We scarcely ever use this. Later you'll see the small sitting room—much cosier.'

Upstairs they bypassed the master bedroom and Jess was rather relieved, not wanting to peep into the private lives of Gareth's parents. There was a large guest room full of heavy, dark furniture, and next door a pretty, smaller bedroom with striped wallpaper, white-painted furniture and a brass bedstead with a rose-printed coverlet that he said had belonged to his sister. 'I do have one,' he told her, looking slightly amused at her surprised look.

'You've never mentioned her, that's all.' Not that there had been any reason for him to do so.

'She's married, living in Perth with her husband. He's a government official in the Internal Affairs Department. And this,' he said, opening a door opposite, 'is where I used to sleep. Come into my parlour.'

He pushed the door wide, and she flashed a sardonic look at him as she stepped into the room.

It still looked like a boy's room, the bookshelves crammed with adventure stories and old geographic magazines, plus a few later thrillers and university text books, and on the wall were several class photographs and some of sports teams. She couldn't even pick his face out from among the rows of boys, except in one that had only four people in it, holding tennis rackets and a large silver cup. The room didn't really give any clues to the man he had become. She looked about, smiled and didn't know what to say.

'Bored?' he asked.

'No, of course not. It's very interesting . . . your house.'

'Spoken like a model guest.'

'I'm doing my best.'

Almost gently he said, 'Yes, you are, aren't you? I scarcely know you in this mood.'

She bit her lip briefly. 'Am I usually so objectionable?'

He shook his head. 'Prickly, though.'

She turned away from him to look out of the window. Through the branches of a great old Moreton Bay fig tree in the garden outside she could see a glimpse of the river.

His hands touched her upper arms, lingered and then pulled her back against him, sliding down to her waist. His mouth warmed the lobe of her ear, then the skin below and the curve of her shoulder.

'Don't,' she said.

He lifted his head and his hand shifted to rest just under her heart, so that she felt it beating against his palm. His chest rose and fell in a sigh, and then he released her.

'Come on, then,' he said. 'Let's complete the guided tour.'

It ended on the ground floor again, in a room lined with books. A solid work desk occupied the bay window, and a dark oak table stood in the middle of the Persian rug on the floor.

'Here,' he said, opening a glass-fronted cabinet. 'Help yourself.'

Reverently she turned the pages of diaries and journals that were two hundred years old, and pored over letters written by men and women who had died long before she was born. She spread some of the material on the table, and together they managed to decipher the often crabbed and faded writing with its strange spellings and archaic phrases. When Gareth said, 'Mother will be expecting us for afternoon tea,' she couldn't believe that it was already four o'clock.

'You're really hooked, aren't you?' he said as they carefully replaced the manuscripts in the cupboard. 'And this is just a hobby?'

'I thought I might write a book,' she said, and then wished that she hadn't. She wasn't at all sure if she was capable of it, and confessing the budding ambition to Gareth made it almost an obligation on her to try.

'What kind of book?'

'A history. I don't know. Something about the area where I live . . . Parramatta's full of history. We still have the old Government House, the Lancer Barracks and some interesting early cottages. Or maybe I'll try and write about the women in the early colony. It's just an idea.'

'I see.' He locked the cabinet with a small silver key. She had the feeling that he didn't believe she was serious. Perhaps he thought she didn't have the talent for it, or the staying power.

The small sitting room was different from the rest of the house, though the corner fireplace was original, with a polished brass fender and hood. It was too warm for a fire, and on the hearth stood an arrangement of berries and dried leaves. The chairs were comfortable, and on a wide shelf under the windows a collection of photographs in silver frames made it much more personal than most of the other rooms.

'Are we late?' she asked as Gareth's father rose from his chair and smiled at her. 'I'm sorry, I was so absorbed in your wonderful collection . . .'

'That's quite all right,' Mrs. Seymour assured her graciously. And her husband added, 'Glad you were able to find something of interest. You're welcome to come and browse any time.'

While his mother poured the tea Gareth asked his father, 'How was the game?' and was given a hole-by-hole description. Stirring sugar into the cup that Mrs. Seymour handed her, Jess looked at the photographs under the window. One looked familiar; it was the same photograph of a fair, pretty girl that Gareth had in his flat, and it sat next to one of him in cap, gown and legal wig.

'Is that Gareth's sister?' she asked. Mrs. Seymour glanced up and said rather repressively, 'No. Fiona is the one at the far end in her wedding dress. That's . . .' She hesitated. 'That was . . . Gareth's fiancée, Angela Mowbray. She died in tragic circumstances. We were all very fond of her.'

Despite a ripple of shock, Jess said conventionally, 'I'm very sorry.'

'It's some years ago now. Time heals,' Mrs. Seymour said in a low voice. 'Though Gareth . . .' She shook her head and sipped at her tea, apparently wishing she had said less.

Jess looked at Gareth, who appeared to be giving all his attention to his father. But as if he felt her gaze, he glanced at her and gave her a faint smile, oddly reassuring. A minute or two later he broke smoothly into his father's discourse. 'We're boring the women-folk, Dad.' Mr. Seymour laughed and turned to Jess. 'I apologise. Golf is a game for fanatics, I'm afraid. You don't play?'

Gareth interjected, 'Not golf.'

Jess's chin lifted, her green eyes gleaming at him. 'Gareth's a bit of a games player himself,' she said pleasantly, 'aren't you?'

She saw the twitch of acknowledgement at the corner of his mouth and felt a quick thrust of exhilaration as his father said, 'He was quite a sportsman at school.'

'I showed her the photos in my room,' Gareth said. 'I don't think she was impressed.'

Dulcetly she said, 'Should I have been?'

He leaned back, his cup and saucer poised in his hands. 'Why do you think I took you in there?'

Butter wouldn't melt in her mouth. Remembering his lips on her shoulder, she said, 'I've no idea.'

His laughing eyes suddenly left hers and blatantly wandered over her body. 'Haven't you?'

She nearly choked on her tea. His mother was looking genteelly disapproving, and his father had begun to smile in a knowing way.

'Do have a biscuit, Jess.' Mrs. Seymour offered a flowered china plate of dainty crackers spread with parsley-topped cream cheese.

Jess accepted gratefully. Mrs. Seymour, apparently determined to quell at the outset any unseemliness at her tea table, took over the conversation.

'You shocked your mother,' Jess said as Gareth drove her home.

'She wasn't shocked.'

'She didn't approve, anyway.'

'Of my behaviour? She'll get over it.'

'Or of me either, I suspect.'

'Don't let it bother you. She hasn't approved of any woman since . . .'

'Since Angela?' Jess asked brittlely into the silence.

'I thought I heard her name mentioned.' His voice was dry.

'I made a mistake. I asked if it was your sister.'

'My mother was very fond of Angela.'

'You must have been, too.'

'I was madly in love with her.'

'I'm sorry,' Jess said miserably. 'I should have shut up about it.'

'It's all right. It doesn't hurt anymore . . . except for an occasional ache at the waste of a young life.'

'How did she die?'

'A virulent kidney infection. It was quite quick.'

'She . . . looks a nice person. I thought she was rather like Claire, at first.'

He glanced at her. 'Yes, Claire often reminded me of her.'

Jess closed her eyes. *Oh, God.* Claire, Angela, two of a kind. Fair and sweet-natured and innocent. His type, no doubt. No wonder he was ambivalent about getting involved with herself. Even when he kissed her she could sense an angry exasperation beneath his passion. Rather obviously she was hardly his ideal woman.

Prig, she thought, and glanced sideways at him, her eyes suddenly inimical. It certainly wouldn't hurt him to be brought down a peg or two. The sexual antagonism that had been held at bay this afternoon came flooding back. She said, 'We could have dinner at my place, if you like. A sort of thank you for this afternoon.'

'I was going to take you out,' he said, 'but that's a nice idea. Are you sure you want to cook?'

'Yes,' she said. 'I'm quite good at it, too. You'd be surprised.'

She turned to watch the buildings flashing by, her mouth curving in a satisfied, rather maleficent little smile.

Chapter Six

He followed her into the kitchen when she went to prepare their meal, asking, 'Can I help?'

'Just keep out of my way,' she answered crisply, and he smiled slightly and leaned on the scrubbed table in the middle of the room.

She took two pork chops from the freezer and put them straight into an oiled pan, browned the outsides, seasoned the meat and placed a lid over it. A lettuce she had bought yesterday would make a salad with tomatoes and asparagus tips; a half pineapple, chopped into pieces, went into a sweet-and-sour sauce to accompany the chops, with frozen ready-cut French fries needing only minutes in hot oil.

'Could I set the table?' Gareth suggested as she shook out the fries.

'I thought we'd eat in the other room.' She reached up to one of the cupboards to get some plates, and when she turned he was eyeing her with undisguised appreciation. She gave him a small, deliberately provocative smile and saw his eyes narrow in return.

'You're not planning to poison me, are you?' he said.

'Why on earth should you think that?' she asked.

'You've been smiling to yourself in that catlike way ever since you invited me to eat with you.'

Smooth as cream, she said, 'What a vivid imagination you have, for a lawyer.'

She put the plates on the table, her shoulder almost brushing his. He didn't make any attempt to get out of the way, merely turning his head so that he could keep studying her face. Jess moved away, a queer kind of excitement gathering in her throat.

She tossed oil and vinegar into the salad and carried the bowl into the other room, setting it in the middle of the low table. Returning to the kitchen, she chose from her small store of drinks, kept cool in what had been the old meat safe, a bottle of white wine made from Barossa Valley grapes. 'You can open this if you like,' she said to Gareth, passing it to him, along with a corkscrew. 'There are glasses in the sitting room.'

He took it from her, his movements leisurely and precise, and went out, and Jess let go a quick breath as the tension suddenly eased.

When he returned she dished up the meal, arranging the food attractively on the plates, with a knife and fork each. 'Very nice,' he said, and she imagined a hint of surprise in his voice.

'No arsenic,' she assured him. She picked up one of the plates and gestured towards the other. 'Can you bring yours?'

The two glasses stood on the coffee table invitingly, with the bottle next to the salad. Jess threw a cushion from one of the chairs to the floor and sank gracefully onto it, curious to know if he would follow suit or prefer a more conventional seat. What he did, once he had cut his meat into pieces and helped himself to salad, was sprawl his long legs on the floor, leaning back against the sofa.

They talked little, only a compliment on her cooking from him and her own acknowledgement, but the meal was leisurely, enhanced by the wine, and as their eyes met in brief, colliding glances she felt the tension grow again, singing vibrantly between them.

He refilled his glass and topped up hers. She took a mouthful of the wine, wiping some from her upper lip with the point of her tongue, and felt her heart thud as his narrowed eyes noted the small action and went hard and brilliant.

She went on slowly eating, and when she had emptied her plate, stood up and stooped to take his.

In the kitchen she slid the plates into the sink and put cheese and biscuits on an oiled board, keeping her mind blank. He was watching for her as she entered the doorway, his wineglass in one long-fingered hand, his eyes intent as she walked across the room and placed the cheeseboard on the table before resuming her seat on the cushion.

Cutting herself a slice of cheese, she laid it carefully on a biscuit, and he said lazily, 'Make one for me?'

She gave him the one in her hand and he reached across the table for it. Jess made herself another and alternated tiny bites with sips of the sharp, cool wine.

He leaned forward to cut himself a hunk of cheese, which he ate without a biscuit, and drained his glass.

'Coffee?' Jess queried as she delicately licked the last crumb from her forefinger.

'No, thanks. Are you having some?'

Jess shook her head, and indicated the cheeseboard. 'More cheese?'

He declined, and she made to remove the board and get up. But Gareth's hand shot out and fastened on her wrist, making her look at him quickly. His eyes had gone a silvery metallic grey and glittered with male challenge. 'Come here, Jess,' he said softly.

She tugged experimentally at her imprisoned wrist and his grip became stronger. 'Come here,' he repeated.

Excitement and anger stirred within her. She shook her head mutely, her glance at him half defiant, half inviting. His jaw thrust forward slightly and his mouth curved in a hard smile. Even so, she was caught unaware by the suddenness and sureness of his movement as he pulled her sideways so that she lost her balance and found herself lying on the softness of the carpet; before she had regained her breath he was kneeling over her, grabbing her other wrist as she took a halfhearted swing at him, and pinning both her hands to the floor.

She looked up into a face grim with a masculine desire to dominate, and said with husky mockery, 'My, my, such macho tactics from a man like you? I'd never have thought it!'

'No?' His voice was cool and steady, only the tiny flare of faintly amused passion at the back of his eyes and the quickened rise and fall of his chest giving any hint of emotion. 'It seems the only method to adopt with a woman like you.'

Her body tensed, but she didn't struggle. She said, flaying herself and him, 'You prefer your women pure

and gentle and nice-mannered, don't you? Like Claire
. . . or Angela.'

'Be quiet, Jess,' he muttered, the light in his eyes
intensifying, and he eased his body down on hers, his
knee insinuated between her thighs. Her startled,
indrawn breath incited him, she could see it in the
tightness of his jaw, in the flush of colour in his face.
Her leg, trapped between his, felt his body heat. He
was scanning her face, his eyes half closing as they
rested on her mouth. She felt her lips parting under the
subtle compulsion of his gaze, before he lowered his
head and claimed them with his own.

His kiss was confident, certain of his welcome, but
unexpectedly gentle. His tongue flicked the edge of her
teeth and then withdrew as the pressure of his lips
increased, coaxing hers further apart until she yielded
completely, relaxing under him, letting her body's soft
contours flow into the harder planes of his. He explored
her mouth thoroughly for a long time, and she recipro-
cated, tasting him, sucking at him, letting her body lie
supine beneath him while their mouths contended in
hungry, restless movements.

Still holding her wrists, he pulled his head away,
arching his body upwards so that he could look down at
her face, sweeping his gaze down to her full breasts and
narrow waist and then, with a small, satisfied smile, to
the junction where they seemed already joined, his
thigh pressing intimately against her; her legs, embrac-
ing his, bent at the knee so that her dress slid away,
exposing smooth, tanned thighs.

He looked back at her flushed face and smiled.
Deliberately, mercilessly watching her, he let her feel
his weight bearing down on her.

Turning sharply away, Jess bit her lip against the

beating waves of desire, and his too-knowledgeable eyes. Her fingers curled into her palms, her wrists throbbing in his hold as the constricted veins found the rush of blood dammed by his grip.

Then one hand was free as he ran his fingers down the side of her neck, lingered while his thumb probed the hammering pulse in the hollow of her throat, and inevitably homed in on the taut curve of her breast. He brought his body down on hers again, slowly kissing her throat, her cheek, teasing the corner of her mouth, running his tongue over her lips and the outline of her ear. Her hand went to her mouth, teeth biting into the knuckles as she tried to exert some control over her rioting senses, and he took it in his and put his lips to her wrist, then opened the fingers to make tiny circles in her palm with his tongue. Turning her head she saw her hand in his, felt his breath on her skin, the weight of his body. His eyes were closed, all his attention concentrated on that erotic contact of mouth and palm, but as if sensing her gaze he lifted his head and looked at her again.

Her eyes were heavy, her skin tightly stretched, every nerve end electrified. Her eyelids drooped, hiding her emotions from him, and then swept up again as she regarded him with a passionate curiosity. Incredible that the cold, supercilious Gareth Seymour could make her respond to him like this, that he could be so aroused by her. Incredible . . . and somehow wildly exciting. For the first time she stirred under him, in some kind of token protest or invitation.

He smiled, and she felt the answering throb and thrust of his desire and made a small, low-pitched sound, her eyes widening and then shutting quickly as her head went back, inviting his mouth on the taut line of her throat . . . his lips, his tongue, the gentle nip of his teeth. And at last he released her wrist and brought both his hands to her breasts, hard, possessive, utterly mind-destroying.

Sighing voluptuously, she flattened her outflung hands against the silky pile of the rug, then brought them back to hold him, running them over the surprisingly fine texture of his hair, taking his head between her palms to guide his mouth back to hers at last, pushing her fingers inside his shirt and stroking skin like raw silk as he slid his arms beneath her and brought her arching explicitly to him.

His arms tensed and he rolled over, still holding her tightly, mouth to mouth and thigh to thigh. He raised his knee between her legs, sweeping his hands down her back, and she lifted her mouth suddenly away from him with a sharp cry of intense pleasure.

His smile was almost a grimace. He turned them once more, so that she lay under him again, and kissed her with bruising, mindless force, and she wrapped her arms about him, kissing him back in a fury of passion.

When he wrenched his mouth away, they were both trembling.

'Here, Jess?' he said roughly. 'Or your bedroom?'

She didn't care. But something about the fact that he had asked sent a distant chill down her spine. With a confused notion that he would despise her if she allowed him to take her there on the floor, as though she was too racked by lust to walk the few paces to a more conventional venue, she drew a deep, unsteady breath and said, 'The bedroom.'

He helped her to her feet and immediately drew her close and kissed her, caressing her back and the upper part of her legs. His fingers found her zipper and slid it down, and with his hand on her bare waist he steered her toward the little room with the wide, brass-ended bed. She stood just inside the door while he closed it behind them, and then his arms came round her, his lips were warm on her nape, and the doubts that had begun to niggle at the edge of her mind were discarded along with the crumpled and abandoned dress left on the floor.

When she woke it was getting light. Gareth still lay sleeping beside her, and the doubts came flocking back, beating cruelly at the barriers she tried to put up against them. Whatever she had foolishly planned yesterday, it wasn't this. She'd had some vague notion of teasing him a little, stringing him along, showing him up in some way, perhaps goading him into losing some of his provoking cool while she hung on to hers. Her machinations had rebounded on her with a vengeance.

She looked at his face, younger in sleep, the fine, straight hair tousled and falling over his forehead. The sheet was down around his waist. He had a lightly muscled, well-shaped torso with a sprinkling of body hair. Her stomach knotted suddenly with unreasoning desire, her hands itching to touch, to stroke, to arouse.

What had happened to her? It wasn't as though he were spectacularly handsome or overpoweringly masculine, wonderfully witty or wildly romantic. If he had showered her with roses, wooed her with champagne and extravagant phrases, the attraction might have been understandable, but he had done none of that. He had criticised her, asked her out only reluctantly after that first impulsive invitation, made it all too clear that he had no wish to take what was between them seriously.

He hadn't even any special bedroom tricks, though he had been a considerate and not unimaginative lover, and, without any need of novel positions or exotic games, had easily wrung from her a reckless, uncontrollable response that left her totally satisfied. And here she was mooning over his sleeping body like a teenager rapt with first love.

She made herself stop looking at him and inched away, lying on her back with her eyes wide open as the dawn chased the shadows from the corners of the high ceiling, determined to rebuild her shattered defences. You've done it again, haven't you? she accused herself. When would she ever learn? Here she had been on the verge of making a satisfactory life for herself, realising that she could make it without a man, that she really didn't need the complications of a love affair, congratulating herself at having resisted Felix and all that his quite formidable powers of persuasion had represented . . . And then she had to succumb just like that to a man who was only using her to help him sublimate his love for her married friend.

Good old Jess, she thought bitterly. The girl who could be relied on to soothe wounded male feelings but who, of course, had none of her own. What feelings could there be under her sophisticated wisecracking, her blasé, expert participation in the games that men and women played, like lyre-birds circling each other, showing off their plumage, pretending indifference and advancing, retreating and finally, sometimes, deciding to mate?

She was tired of the games, didn't want to be a

participant anymore. And most of all she didn't relish being the temporary solace for Gareth's bruised heart. That had definitely not been part of the plan last night.

Perhaps it wasn't too late to retrieve her independence and some pride. If he thought this was more than a one-night-stand she would soon disabuse him of the notion, anyway. He probably imagined it was something she did all the time, in any case. Let him think so. Just so long as this wasn't allowed to go any further. She didn't *need* another man in her life, especially one who thought of her as a useful stopgap, an available woman to take the place of one who wasn't.

He didn't stir when she slipped stealthily out of the bed and went to the bathroom with her clothes. She showered and dressed, left out a clean towel, a disposable razor and a new toothbrush still in its cellophane packet on the vanity top, and then went to the kitchen. She had cleared the dishes they had left the previous night, and drunk two cups of strong black coffee before she heard him in the shower.

By the time he entered the kitchen, dressed in trousers and shirt, the table was set for two and Jess was frying bacon and eggs.

'Good morning,' he said, dropping a kiss on her nape. His hands came round her waist, but she resisted his efforts to pull her against him, and after a moment he moved away.

'Can I do anything?' he asked her.

'Make some toast, if you like,' she said indifferently. 'The bread's there, and the toaster. How do you like your egg?'

'However it comes,' he said easily.

She felt him watching her as she slid the bacon and

eggs onto warmed plates on the table. He had buttered the toast and found a plate to put it on.

Avoiding his eyes, she sat down and motioned for him to do the same. 'Help yourself to coffee when you want it,' she offered abruptly.

He took the chair, picked up his knife and fork and said gently, 'Not a morning person, Jess?'

Looking up, she saw him smiling, in his eyes a warmth that she had never seen before, which did something peculiar to her equilibrium.

'Are *you?*' she fenced.

He shrugged. 'More or less.'

'Lucky you.' She turned her attention to what was on her plate, but it was a few seconds before he began using the knife and fork in his hands.

Jess didn't linger over coffee, and when she began clearing up he helped her, drying quite efficiently as she washed the few plates and cups.

'Thank you,' she said when they had finished, her voice clipped.

'Want me to go?' he asked her quietly.

'Please yourself.' Her eyes met his momentarily and skittered away.

'I had hoped to please *you.*'

'Oh, you did,' she said carelessly, 'as I'm sure you know.' She looked at him sideways, characteristically mocking. 'Do you actually need reassurance, Gareth?'

A faint spark lit his eyes. 'No. Your reactions last night were fairly unequivocal. Unlike this morning. What's the matter, Jess? Afraid you might have given away too much? Embarrassed because I've seen you losing control of yourself, because you finally let yourself go . . . in my arms?'

Her heart beating uncomfortably, she said, 'Spending a night in my bed doesn't give you any right to psychoanalyse me.'

'I wasn't supposing it gave me any rights at all. But I don't appreciate being treated like a leper after a night of . . . intimacy. I'd have thought it would give us a basis of communication at least.'

'You've got a fancy way of putting it, lawyer-man.' She gave him a deliberately challenging look from under her lashes. 'I'd say we communicate very well— on a certain level.'

Grimly he said, 'Yes, we do. It was always there, wasn't it, Jess? And now we know for sure. But is that all you want?'

The question shook her off balance. She wasn't able to articulate what she wanted. More, yes, but she didn't trust herself—or him—enough to try and explain the complications of her feelings. Instead, she fell back on habit and the reflexes of years of self-preservation and said with ironical nonchalance, '*Is* there anything more?'

His face didn't change, but in his eyes something died, leaving them cold and critical. He thrust his hands into his pockets and rocked back a little on his heels, looking at her with slow deliberation. Her pose was provocation in itself: her hands resting on the bench behind her, thrusting her breasts into prominence and her pelvis forward, her legs casually crossed. He inspected her almost insultingly, and when his eyes returned to her face the coldness was giving way to angry desire. 'Perhaps not,' he said, and began coming towards her.

She had a sudden impulse to say, No, I didn't mean it! But at the same time a stirring of sensual excitement locked the words in her throat.

When he reached her she tried to get away, but he caught her arm, her waist, and though she pushed at him he simply blocked her movement and lifted her into his arms.

She resisted all the way to the bedroom, and even after he threw her down on the still rumpled bed, panting, straining against him silently, writhing away from his imprisoning hands, but she knew it only increased the excitement for each of them. When he had stripped her and they were both breathing harshly from the physical exertion of his steely determination and her obstinate refusal to yield to what they both wanted, she lay exhausted against the pillows, watching him unbuckle his belt, her eyes half closed and glimmering.

'Your shirt's torn,' she told him with husky satisfaction, and he grinned down at her as he hauled it off and dropped it onto the floor.

'Bitch,' he said, making the word sound like a caress. He lay beside her and gathered her into his arms. 'Beautiful, beautiful bitch,' he said against her heated skin as she arched to his embrace and dug her nails into his back.

The tiny, half-moon indentations were still there afterwards; she saw them as he half sat to draw the sheet up. Her hands on his shoulders, she leaned forward and began kissing the marks, her lips enjoying the slightly salty taste of his skin, the smooth texture of it.

'Have you scarred me for life?' he asked.

'I hope so!' Jess answered passionately.

'Fierce, aren't you?' He laughed and twisted round, pinning her to the mattress and displacing the sheet again so that it wound about his loins and left her exposed to the waist. His eyes flickered over her, dwelling on her breasts, and his hand made to pull the covering away altogether. She clutched at the linen, and he looked up at her face and grinned. 'A bit late to be shy,' he jeered gently.

'I'm not shy!' she said, disclaiming the image of a shrinking violet that the word evoked.

'Modest, then. Unexpectedly so.'

'Oh?' Almost ready to take offence, she looked up into his eyes.

'You're such a self-assured lady,' he told her. 'And you have a superb figure . . . Why do you want to hide it from me?'

Hostile, she said, 'It's *my* body. *I* decide who sees it, and when.'

'You're still determined to keep the barriers up, aren't you?' He sounded slightly irritated. 'I'm trying to make *love* to you, woman . . . not wage some sort of battle campaign.'

'Is there much difference?' she retorted, remembering the fight that had culminated in that violently passionate coupling.

'Perhaps not for you,' he said coolly.

'What do you mean?'

'Nothing.' He was angry but controlled.

She opened her mouth, lifting her head off the pillow, ready to hurl words at him, a jibe or a challenge. But a hard hand thrust her back again and slid to her throat, the thumb pushing up her chin. 'Shut up, Jess,' he said. 'Don't spoil it.'

His mouth silenced her definitively, but she wouldn't kiss him back, even though heat was stirring again in her stomach and her limbs went slack as his lips continued caressing and probing impatiently.

At last he broke the kiss and laid his head beside hers, muttering, 'Damn you, Jess.' But there was reluctant humour and admission of a kind of defeat in his voice, in the wry smile he slanted at her.

She turned her head and fastened her teeth on his earlobe, laughing at his sharply indrawn breath. He twisted suddenly, dragging her with him so that she lay on the length of his body, and his fingers raked into her short hair, holding back her head. Then his mouth opened against her throat, his teeth grazing the flesh, a small, less than serious, sensual threat.

His hands slipped about her throat as his mouth left it to fasten on her breast, and then his fingers followed his mouth and went further until they reached her hips. She lowered her head to his shoulder and began nibbling at it, warily gentle, and she felt him tense and then give a long, gratified sigh. His hands tightened on her hips and shifted her body upwards, sliding on his, then down, a repeated, rhythmic invitation, until she could stand it no longer and demanded, with her legs, her body, her exploring, begging hands, that he end the sweet torture. He did, engulfing her at last in a blaze of shared pleasure almost too intense to be borne.

She was dizzy when he had eased her back onto the pillow, whispering, 'Okay?' She nodded silently, her eyes flickering open, her face still nakedly reflecting slowly fading passion. 'God, Jess!' he said, his voice thickening. 'Are you always like that?'

Her eyes winced away from his.

He groaned a curse. 'I know, I shouldn't have said it. Forget it.'

Her face remained averted, and he turned it gently with his palm laid along her cheek. 'Jess, don't leave me out in the cold again. The question was out of order. I admit it, and apologise as abjectly as I know how.' His voice was soft and persuasive, and his lips nuzzled at her throat, her temples, the smooth, hollowed skin below her ear. When they reached her lips she passively allowed his touch, but the steady, warm insistence of his kiss melted her in the end, and she began to return it, slowly at first, almost sleepily, and then with increasing fervour.

He threw the sheet aside again and traced lazy, erotic patterns on her skin with his fingers while his mouth still tantalised hers. Her breathing quickened, and she began caressing him, too, running her fingertips over his shoulderblades and down his spine.

When she felt him move against her, she pulled her mouth from his and regarded him from narrowed eyes. Her voice low and teasing, she said, 'You can't—again!'

'Can't I?' His eyes gleamed a challenge. He put his hands on either side of her face and brought his lips again to hers. Brushing the softness of her smiling mouth, he muttered, 'Just watch me try!'

It was after midday before they got up again, and this time they showered together, soaping each other and taking a long time over it, drying themselves while watching each other, their eyes exchanging admiring, laughing, delighted messages.

They realised that they were hungry, and went out to eat, ordering an enormous meal which neither of them finished. Afterwards they drove through the city and out to the coast along the South Head Road. There they sat for a long time overlooking the Pacific and admiring the twin white domes and central tower of the Macquarie lighthouse, a replica of the first Australian lighthouse built on the same spot by one of the early governors. The cliffs were high and sheer, the waves thundering against them and spuming almost to the top, but nearer the horizon the sea was blue and tranquil, with a fine purple line at its edge where it met the paler blue of the sky.

'Imagine sailing down the coast there in the eighteenth century,' Jess said, 'along those cliffs and into the Heads, and finding the most magnificent harbour in the world inside them.'

'I wonder how the convicts felt about it.'

'Scared, of course. But among the men, anyway, there were some who took it as an opportunity to start over again.'

'What about the women?' Gareth asked. 'Mary Reiby was pretty astute by all accounts, and a name to be reckoned with in the business world of the old colony.'

'A few women did very well for themselves. Mostly through men, though. It was harder for them. They had to do everything through some man—a husband, a protector, an official who took pity on them . . . or was willing to accept a certain sort of payment in kind. Did you know what Mary Reiby was transported for?'

'Theft?' Gareth guessed.

'Stealing a horse, it was called. She was a thirteen-year-old child and she "stole" a ride on the local squire's cob. And for that she got seven years. Which was actually a life sentence, since she had no means of getting home again to her family. The government didn't feel itself responsible for repatriating prisoners who had served their sentences.'

'You're sounding quite bitter on poor Mary's behalf.' He paused. 'Are you still going to write that book?'

'You don't think I can, do you?'

'Do you really want to?'

Reluctant, as always, to commit herself, she said, 'I'm thinking about it.' She returned her gaze to the white-edged breakers running in lines from the sea. The cliffs had withstood their battering for thousands of years, but one day they would crumble before the relentless water. She could do with some of that determination. The early settlers must have had it, both the willing and the unwilling ones—those who had not gone to the wall in that harsh world of the lash and the leg-iron.

Then came the idea, springing into life fully formed, as though her subconscious had been chewing it over and was now ready to present it to her conscious mind. *Not a history, there are plenty of those and I'm not really qualified. A novel—a novel about a woman, a convict woman.*

That, too, had been done, she supposed. But not, surely, in exactly the way she wanted to do it. For some time she had been pursuing brief references to a particular woman, Beth Starke, who had arrived on a convict transport, turned up in the records of the notorious Women's Factory at Parramatta and later married a free settler. It had been exciting to find the second reference to her and intriguing to discover a third. The documents in which Beth's name appeared were far too lacking in detail for any clear picture of the woman to emerge. But a fictionalised Beth could be fleshed out with imagination and minor details from the lives of other, typical female convicts into a believable character.

'Jess?' Gareth's hand on her shoulder turned her to face him. 'Where did you go?'

'Back to the eighteenth century,' she admitted, her eyes shining.

He searched her face, faintly smiling. 'Was there a man there?'

Jess laughed, and her tongue flicked briefly between her teeth. 'Lots,' she said. 'But I was thinking of a woman, actually.'

His eyes on her mouth, he said, 'Good.'

His hand tightened on her shoulder, drawing her close. Blanking out thought, she lifted her mouth for his kiss, and it was long and slow and very satisfying. Some time later he said, 'It's getting dark. We should head back.'

On the way she tried to repeat to herself all the cogent arguments of that morning, preparing to tell him that they weren't embarking on a continuing sexual relationship. She should say, Thanks, it was nice, that's it, and good-bye. Then he put out his hand and caught her fingers in his and raised them to his lips, and all her resolution melted in heedless, ridiculous longing. She made an inarticulate sound, half laugh and half moan, and he glanced at her and smiled, and she smiled stupidly back, lost, swept away, hopelessly caught in a whirlpool of aching desire. Not yet, her heart whispered to her rapidly disintegrating will. Not just yet. One more time, she thought, knowing she was kidding herself, the cynical side of her jeering in the background that she was hooked and might as well admit it. She was in too deep already, would find herself playing the passive little woman to Gareth's masterful male, drifting into a dead-end affair, waiting for him to be the one to end it.

They bought chips and fried tidbits in bags, and when they reached her house she put on a record and they lounged on the floor and ate straight out of the bags, swapping batter-coated morsels and licking their fingers afterwards.

She stuffed the bags into her rubbish bin and made coffee while Gareth put on another record. When she brought the cups in he was on the sofa. He moved over to make room and she obeyed the mute gesture and sat beside him.

Putting down his cup, he took her hand, kissing the palm as he had once before. Her fingers quivered in his and she bit hard on her lower lip.

His eyes were hard but lit with a flame of desire. 'Jess,' he said, 'I want to stay the night again.'

'Yes,' she said, barely breathing. She looked at their joined hands and experienced a strange stab of psychic pain. Swaying towards him, she laid her bent head against his shoulder and began mindlessly kissing his fingers, her lips feverish. She could feel his heart thudding beneath her cheek, and when he said hoarsely, 'Jess!' she threw back her head with a smile of triumph because she knew that the fire that threatened to consume her was equally fierce and dangerous within him.

Chapter Seven

So they became lovers. He spent most weekends at her house, and often weeknights, too. At Christmas he wanted her to come to Karunja with him and they quarrelled because she refused. He told her that he could have understood if she had wanted to go to her own family, and at that she laughed and said she hadn't been home for years and she certainly wasn't going to make an exception this year. She had sent her usual present to her parents, and received one from her mother signed with love from Mum, Dad and the boys, but she didn't believe in that. Probably her mother had bought it in secret and dispatched it furtively, and she didn't know what happened to her yearly gifts. Possibly her father threw them away.

She didn't tell any of this to Gareth, merely saying stubbornly that if she preferred to spend the so-called festive season alone, it was none of his business. She certainly didn't want to be at his family home, with his parents and sister speculating about their relationship and watching their every move.

In the end he gave up, but he came late on Christmas night and gave her a present, a recording of a Greig Concerto that she had mentioned she had once owned but had lost.

'I haven't bought anything for you,' she said, almost sulkily. She hadn't intended to start exchanging presents; it argued an intimacy that she wasn't ready for.

'It doesn't matter,' he told her. 'I just wanted to give you pleasure.'

She put on the record and they listened to it right through before he pulled her into his arms and kissed her and, eventually, made love to her.

They spent most of his annual leave together. On New Year's Day, with thousands of other Sydneysiders, they found a spot overlooking the harbour to watch the start of the annual Sydney to Hobart yacht race. The water was crowded with competitors, wellwishers and sightseers in boats of every size and colour, even surfsailers darting in amongst them. Jess sunbaked in shorts and a brief top and laughingly chided Gareth for wearing a hat.

'I don't have your gorgeous olive skin,' he retorted, running his finger along her smooth tanned thigh. 'Do you fancy me with a red and peeling nose?'

It probably wouldn't make any difference, she thought, because she fancied him so much that even the touch of his finger had set her alight. The power he had over her emotions fascinated and frightened her.

Sometimes after a date she spent the night at his apartment, and she would wake to see him putting on his shirt or knotting his tie, his eyes enjoying her tousled sleepiness and the wanton disorder of his bed, before he bent to kiss her lingeringly and went away to his office.

She knew he pictured her lazing away the morning before making the bed and letting herself out of the flat. But in reality she hardly waited for the door to close behind him before she was up and showering. She would have a quick cup of coffee and be on her way within half an hour of Gareth's leaving.

Because she had another obsession. Her novel, once she had conceived the basic idea, had quickly taken on a life of its own. She regularly pored through books and documents either at home or in libraries to give her the turbulent background to the plot, and spent hours at the typewriter getting it onto paper, gradually winning the battle to improve her typing. She had torn up some of the pages several times, and rewritten the entire first chapter as often. She still wasn't totally satisfied with her beginning, but the rest of the novel was crowding in on her consciousness, and she felt an almost superstitious need to get it down before the life of the story faded. Later she would go back over it all and rewrite it yet again. And she hoped that by then her typing would have improved, too.

Each day she put away the typewritten sheets in a drawer so that the evidence of her activity was hidden, and when Gareth came he saw only the covered typewriter. Sometimes she noticed him looking at it, but he didn't comment.

Pietro phoned her towards the end of February and asked, 'Are you still interested in writing a book, Jess?'

Cautiously she answered, 'Well . . . yes.' And waited.

'I've met a charming lady who is an editor for a publishing house,' he told her. 'She is looking for books on Australian history . . . both fiction and nonfiction. Would you like to meet her?'

'Would she like to meet me?' Jess countered. 'I mean, she may only want established writers.'

'No, no. She is very keen to develop new local authors. If I bring her to see you, would you have something to show to her?'

'Yes,' Jess said, taking the plunge. 'Yes I would. I do. But it may not be any good. . . .'

'Then let her judge, hmm? It's her job, after all.'

'Yes, all right.'

When they had arranged a day and time, she was surprised at how apprehensive she was. She went over and over all that she had done, one minute thinking it inexpressibly bad and the next convinced that it was at least better than some of the published works she had read. Once or twice she experienced a thrill of pleasure at a passage which she felt had come out exactly right and conveyed the atmosphere, the emotion, that she had been trying to portray. Yet other paragraphs which had pleased her when she wrote them seemed flat and lifeless.

She had always read widely and with a fairly critical eye, which must, she supposed, help. But trying to assess her own work was rather like being a mother judging a baby contest in which her own offspring was a contender.

Pietro, she gathered, was taking the woman to lunch, and they would visit her afterwards. She couldn't suppose it was the way editors normally worked. Pietro had asked a favour on her behalf, making the meeting semisocial, not entirely business. She wondered whether the editor minded. But then few women would object to lunching with Pietro, even at the price of having to pass judgement on the amateur work of one of his friends. One thing Jess was sure of—doing Pietro favours wouldn't extend to expressing a spurious interest if her writing was hopelessly bad.

Vivienne Tapper turned out to be a charming person: fortyish, intelligent and with a sparkling sense of humour. Her brown hair waved prettily back from a high forehead, her clothes were casual but smart, and as she sat on Jess's sofa and crossed neat ankles, Jess couldn't help noticing that she had particularly nice legs. That fact had obviously not escaped Pietro's attention either, and Jess hid a smile as she saw his appreciative glance and Vivienne's careful avoidance of it.

'Well,' Vivienne invited when the preliminaries were over, 'what do you have to show me?'

Jess produced the folder that held the six chapters she had written, and handed them over diffidently, even now suffering a strong desire to hide them from all eyes but her own.

Vivienne opened the folder and enquired, 'Is this the first draft?'

'Not exactly.' Jess hesitated. 'But it isn't the final copy. It still needs working on.'

Vivienne's friendly brown eyes rested on her thoughtfully. 'Well, that's the right approach,' she said. 'Writers who are totally satisfied with their own work are usually not as good as they think they are. You *will* double space the final version, won't you? And use a heavier paper. This bank stuff is flimsy. Get some good bond.'

'Yes,' Jess said, mentally taking note. She must get a book from the library on setting out a typescript, she decided. Perhaps she should subscribe to a writers' magazine. If she wanted to be taken seriously, she ought to learn the rudiments of presenting her work, anyway, and something about the craft of writing.

Vivienne turned her attention to the first page, but had skimmed only half a dozen when she closed the folder decisively. Jess's heart sank.

'Do you have a carbon or a photocopy of this?' Vivienne asked crisply.

'Yes.' She was thankful that she had at least known that much.

'Then may I take this back to the office with me?'

'Yes, of course. But don't feel obliged to . . .'

'I'm not obliged to do anything.' A quick smile took any sting out of the words. 'I would like to read the rest before I pass an opinion, that's all. What about a synopsis?'

'What?' Jess was puzzled.

Patiently Vivienne said, 'Do you have a synopsis? A brief résumé of how the rest of the story will go?'

'Only handwritten notes on what I plan to include in each chapter, I'm afraid.'

'Type them out, would you, and send them to me? I'll give you a card with the address. . . . Three to six pages is all I need. And it doesn't tie you down to finishing the book in exactly that way. It just gives me an idea if you are likely to be able to sustain the story line.'

After they had left Jess found herself alternating between hopeful excitement and gloomy scepticism. She took out the notes she had made on the further development of the story and began to type, sorting them into coherent sentences as she went. It took her the rest of the afternoon, which was just as well, she reflected as she sealed the envelope. She didn't think she would have been able to concentrate on the next chapter if she had begun it today.

Something in the notes had triggered a memory. In the papers at Karunja there had been a reference to a young woman being punished for some misdemeanour by being placed in the stocks. Deciding she might use a version of the incident, she made a mental resolution to get another look at those documents. Now that she had a more detailed view in mind of what her story line was to be, it would be much easier to home in on specific, useful references.

When she asked him, Gareth looked faintly surprised but said, 'Of course. Whenever it suits you.'

Anxious not to lose time, she asked if he could take her out to the house the next evening.

'I'll check with my parents.' He used her phone while she busied herself in the kitchen, not wanting to seem to be listening. He came in a few minutes later and said, 'We're invited for dinner, okay?'

Embarrassed, Jess said, 'I didn't mean to impose myself on your family. . . .'

'Don't be silly. They want to see you again.'

His father might, Jess conceded silently. She was doubtful about his mother's feelings, though.

However, Mrs. Seymour's manner towards her seemed rather less chilly than the last time they had met, and the dinner turned out to be quite pleasant.

Afterwards Jess and Gareth repaired again to the bookroom, and she took out a spiral-bound notebook and a pen as he removed the material she had asked for from the cabinet.

'You look very businesslike,' he commented, intrigued.

'I know you think I'm just a pretty face. . . .'

'I think nothing of the kind. You're a very complex person, Jess. Are you going to tell me what you want these for?'

'I told you, I might write a book.'

'Might . . .' he repeated, watching her leaf carefully through one of the journals to find the part she wanted. As she spread the pages and uncapped her pen he said softly, 'You've started it, haven't you?'

'How did you know?' For an instant she suspected him of snooping in the drawer where she had placed her unfinished manuscript, but of course he hadn't. If he had wanted to look he would have done so openly, or asked point-blank.

'You know exactly what you're after, this time,' he said. 'You didn't before. You were just browsing. What's it going to be about?'

'I don't want to talk about it,' she said. 'Do you mind?'

He looked at her silently for a moment, then shrugged. 'Okay.'

He wandered away while she scribbled, standing with his hands thrust into his pockets, so quiet that after a time she forgot about him. She was immersed in the past, her brain picking up detail after detail that fitted into the complicated mosaic of the story she was creating. Each thread seemed to lead into another, so that when Mrs. Seymour tapped on the door and looked in to ask if they'd like coffee, Jess was startled to realise how late it was.

'We'll be with you in a few minutes, Mother,' Gareth said, straightening from where he had been leaning against a wall of books.

'You can come back some other time,' he reminded Jess as his mother closed the door again. 'I'm getting a bit tired of being ignored.'

'Sorry,' she said. Had he been standing watching her all that time? But he had a book in his hand, which he fitted back onto the shelf behind him.

'Are you?' he said, strolling towards her as she began to gather up the material she had been using. 'You can prove it to me later,' he suggested.

She slanted him a smile full of sensual challenge, and he reached out a seemingly negligent hand to pull her to him, planting a hard kiss on her mouth. His hands sliding to her waist, he said, 'In fact you can start now.'

She arched away, pushing against him, but he found her mouth again and held her until he had made her respond. When he let her go they were both slightly breathless, and his eyes rested brilliantly on her moist, swollen mouth.

'Your parents will be waiting,' she said, turning to stack the journals with shaking hands.

The following day she had a phone call from Vivienne Tapper. 'Can you come in and see me? I'd like to talk to you about your book.'

What the talk amounted to was that although the manuscript suffered from what Vivienne called 'a few beginner's faults,' she basically liked it, liked the writing style provided Jess was willing to 'polish it a bit,' and wanted to talk about a contract.

Jess had to suppress her initial dismay when she

learned that Vivienne wanted her to discard almost the entire first chapter on which she had worked so hard. But she quickly grasped the point that the careful scene-setting delayed the onset of the story itself, and she saw that the other minor criticisms the editor had were the result of long experience and a very good eye for redundant phrases and unnecessary exposition.

Clasping the manuscript with Vivienne's pencilled comments on it, she walked out of the publisher's office with a sense of triumph. Of course there was a long way to go, but it seemed she was on the right track.

Grateful for Pietro's intervention, she decided that he deserved to hear the news first. She slipped into a phone booth and dialled his office.

Delighted, he congratulated her and insisted on meeting her for a celebratory drink. The drink became two, and then three, and in the end he gave her dinner before driving her home.

Gareth was on the doorstep, his car at the gate.

'You were expecting him?' Pietro asked softly as he stopped the car.

Jess shook her head. 'No, not tonight.' Gareth had said nothing, although it was not unusual now for him to drop by unexpectedly.

'He looks . . . not pleased,' Pietro said, giving her a quizzical look before he got out and went round to open her door.

She pushed down a twinge of guilt. Gareth had no right to be annoyed. He could hardly expect her to be waiting for him every time he decided to make a casual call on her. Anyway, she refused to allow her exciting day to be spoiled.

So she greeted him gaily as Pietro put his hand on her

waist and accompanied her to the door. Gareth stood aside, and Jess handed Pietro her key.

Perversely, when the older man offered to leave she insisted on his coming in for coffee, and he shot a shrewd, amused glance from her defiant smile to Gareth's impassive face and accepted, raising a dark brow at her with a hint of sardonic understanding.

Jess went into the kitchen and came back with a tray holding three glasses and a bottle of sparkling white wine. 'Shall we open this first?' she suggested. 'We can make a start on it while I brew up the coffee.'

'What's the occasion?' Gareth enquired with a slight edge to his voice.

'Jess has sold her book,' Pietro explained, taking the bottle from her to open it.

'Oh, not quite!' Jess objected. 'But I've been asked to sign a contract.'

'Well,' Gareth said after a moment. 'Congratulations.'

Pietro filled the glasses that Jess had put on the sideboard and handed them one each. Taking his own, he said, 'To Jess, and her future as an author.'

'Certainly, to Jess,' Gareth murmured, raising his glass, but when she met his eyes they were cold. 'I don't know how you've had the time,' he said. 'I thought it was only in the beginning stage.'

'It is, virtually,' Jess told him. 'But they're willing to give me a contract on the basis of the first few chapters, and provided the rest is up to standard they'll publish it.'

'So you ran into Pietro and decided to celebrate?' Gareth concluded.

Rather wickedly, Pietro said, 'No. She phoned me to

tell me the good news, and I naturally suggested that we honour her success.'

Gareth looked at him glacially. 'Naturally,' he agreed.

About to explain that Pietro had introduced her to the editor who had persuaded the publisher to accept her work, Jess decided to hold her tongue. Gareth's reaction had dashed her a little, for he didn't seem exactly overjoyed at her news. It was almost as though she had disappointed him by not living down to his expectations. He probably still thought she wouldn't finish the project in spite of her present enthusiasm and the fillip given her by the promise, however conditional, of publication. Well, she owed Gareth no explanations; he didn't have any claims on her. Let him think what he liked.

Gareth said, looking at Pietro, 'And how is Claire?'

A shadow crossed the other man's face. 'I'm a little worried about her,' he confessed. 'She is happy about the baby, of course, but she often seems pale and not as well as I would like.'

Jess suffered a pang of guilt. She had seen nothing of her friend for weeks, although they had spoken on the telephone. Absorbed in her book and her affair with Gareth, she had spared little time for anything else since Christmas. This afternoon she had scarcely mentioned Claire to her stepfather, only saying in passing how thrilled Claire and Scott had been at starting a family, taking for granted that Claire was still radiant and healthy. Pietro, perhaps loath to disturb her own radiance, had not said anything then about feeling there was something wrong. Now, however, he looked distinctly troubled.

'I'm sorry,' Jess said. 'I was caught up in my own concerns, and she seemed so well when I last saw her. . . . But lots of women suffer from morning sickness, don't they? That's probably all it is.'

Pietro nodded. 'I hope so. But I have suggested to Scott that she should perhaps see a specialist. Only Claire says we're fussing over nothing. She can be very stubborn, that girl.'

'If she needs to see a specialist, Scott will get her to one,' Jess assured him. '*He's* a very stubborn man.'

The look Pietro shot her had the same speculative gleam she had seen before when she mentioned his son-in-law. Looking right back, she said, 'I've been friends with Scott a long time.'

His eyes searched hers a moment longer. Then he said simply, 'Yes,' and she knew he had accepted the frank message in the gaze she turned to him. He raised his glass to take a sip of wine.

Gareth, she realised, wasn't missing anything. He looked relaxed enough as he adopted an elegant sprawl across the sofa, but his pose was too still, his eyes too hooded.

'I'll check on the coffee,' she said, escaping to the kitchen.

When she carried the cups in the men were conducting a very civilised conversation, but the glimmer of amusement in Pietro's eyes was more pronounced, and Gareth, although hiding it under a veneer of good manners, was decidedly out of temper.

When Pietro offered to go, she went to the door with him, regarding his pleased expression with suspicion and finally demanding in a low voice, 'What have you been up to?'

He looked down at her and laughed. 'My dear Jess, when a man gets to my age, it is irresistible to play along a little when one as young as my friend Gareth gets it into his head to be jealous. Forgive me. Shall I go back and explain to him that we are just great friends, you and I?'

'No, you will not!' Jess said, unable to resist laughing back at him. 'You know it would only make it much worse.'

'It is serious, between you?'

Jess shook her head, refusing to be drawn any further.

He smiled at her in his engaging, sexy, Italian way, and bent to put his mouth to her lips with extreme lightness. 'It is tempting,' he said very softly, 'to send you back to him looking thoroughly, unmistakably kissed.'

His eyes asked an impudent question, his finger already under her chin to turn her face up, but she clasped his hand and removed it, smiling and shaking her head. 'You,' she said, 'have caused quite enough trouble for one night.'

'Me?' He was injured innocence personified. 'Dear girl, I have done nothing except perhaps make him realise—if he was not already aware—what a very attractive and talented young woman you are. If I were only ten years younger . . .' he added wistfully. 'But never mind . . . And don't worry. You will make it up, and he will appreciate all the more what a lucky man he is.'

When she went back into the room Gareth was sitting just as she had left him, staring into his empty coffee cup. He looked up as she stopped in the door-way, and they exchanged a long, wordless glance, wary on her side, unreadable on his.

'Shall I go, too?' he asked her at last.

Unfair to put it to her like that. What was she supposed to do, she wondered resentfully, beg him to stay?

'Whatever you like.' She went into the room, holding out her hand for his cup.

He straightened and passed it to her. But as she was walking away he suddenly got up and took it from her again, putting it down on the table while he held her wrist and twisted her to face him. And then he was kissing her with a fierce, inescapable passion that set her blood roaring and turned her bones to liquid fire.

Her pride demanded that she put up a token strug-gle, but she couldn't hide the rising excitement in her eyes, the wild flush of desire in her face, the telltale, sensual signs with which her body told him that she wanted him. He carried her to the bed, threw her onto its softness and took her almost immediately, and her panting, frustrated protests were all too soon trans-formed into sobbing gasps of fulfillment. It wasn't until they had come together again in a gentler, more leisurely way, with her complete cooperation this time, that he asked, 'What the hell were you doing with Pietro, anyway?'

She laughed, low, satisfied and with a husky note of triumph. Her eyes gleamed at him seductively. 'He said you were jealous.'

'Wasn't that what you wanted?' he countered. He took her wrist and forced it back onto the pillow up above her head, and began kissing her inner arm, his lips travelling from her trapped wrist to the crook of her elbow. 'Go on, admit it,' he murmured between kisses.

Jess shook her head. 'It wasn't intentional. Not on my part, anyway. Pietro was playing games, though.'

'And you,' he accused, lifting his head, remembered anger in his eyes. He took up her imprisoned hand and softly bit at the tip of a finger.

'No,' she denied. 'But I did think you deserved it. I was angry with you.'

'Why?'

'I hoped you'd be pleased . . . about my book being accepted.'

'Of course I'm pleased!'

'Well,' she said dryly, 'you scarcely showed it.'

Exasperation was in his face. 'What sort of a chance did you give me?' he demanded. 'Pietro told me, not you. You'd rushed to him first with the news, celebrated with him already. Telling me was apparently an afterthought.'

'Pietro put me in touch with the publisher,' she said simply. 'That's why I told him before anyone.'

He stared down at her, enlightenment in his eyes. He said slowly, 'I see. Why the hell didn't you say so in the first place?'

'Does it matter? I don't really know. You were being so cool about it, I thought . . .'

'That I didn't deserve to know. I'm truly sorry if my lack of enthusiasm spoiled your triumph for you, Jess. I was thrown by your going to Pietro with it first.'

Surprise kept her silent for a moment. 'You mean . . . hurt?' she asked huskily, her eyes questioning.

'Okay,' he admitted with slight grimness, 'hurt. Satisfied?'

'Only because I was hurt, too,' she said, 'by your casual attitude.'

'Well, well ... . Confession time?' he taunted. 'I thought we agreed we were both impregnable?'

'That was a long time ago.'

'Yes,' he agreed soberly. 'What a long time ago that was.'

He turned suddenly, slipping his arm about her and lying on his back with her held in the crook of his arm, her cheek resting on his chest. 'What are we going to do about it?'

She recalled that he had asked that question before. And in the end had taken no notice of her answer. This time she didn't answer at all, preferring a drowsy silence while she listened to the steady beat of his heart and let him stroke her hair and softly run his finger along the line of her neck and shoulder and down her arm.

She was almost asleep when he said, 'Jess . . . I want to get married.'

For a moment her heart stopped. I'm dreaming it, she thought in panic. But she wasn't. Taking refuge in flippancy, she said, 'Who to?'

He moved, waking her up thoroughly, and gripped her shoulders. 'I'm serious, damn you!'

Her startled eyes met his. 'Marriage is a serious business,' she said weakly.

'*Jess!*' His hands tightened threateningly, wanting to shake her.

'You can't mean it!'

'For heaven's sake! Do you think I'd be proposing to you if I didn't mean it?' His face changing, he said somewhat cynically, 'I don't have your ex-husband's money, of course, or Scott Carver's looks. But I live very comfortably on my income—and you can't have Scott, anyway.'

'I don't *want* Scott!' she snapped. 'And I don't give a damn about your income.'

He scanned her face, his eyes hard and almost suspicious. 'Well, let's get one thing straight. My wife is not going to live on another man's money.'

Instantly antagonistic, she said coldly, 'You're taking a lot for granted, aren't you? Just because you've decided to make an honest woman of me, am I supposed to fall at your feet?'

'Don't I wish!' he said derisively. 'Stop trying to make a fight of it, Jess.'

'I am not . . . !'

'Yes, you are. You always do whenever things start getting emotional. You're scared stiff of feeling anything.'

'Don't talk rubbish!'

'What happened, Jess?' he said, suddenly gentle. 'Why are you so terrified of letting anyone get too close?'

'Oh, come on!' she said, her face sardonic. 'You know what happened.'

'Your marriage? Was it that bad?'

She smiled, brittle and uncaring. 'No, actually it was fun. Only then it stopped being fun, so we called it a day. It was all very amicable . . . We're really quite friendly, Denny and I. And he's been . . . generous.'

She wriggled away from his hold and lay back on the pillow, one arm thrown casually behind her head.

He looked at her searchingly, and she gazed back with a bland face, a slight smile on her lips.

'I don't believe it was as simple as that,' he said. 'I think somewhere along the line you were badly hurt.'

Her shoulders lifted in a small, indifferent shrug. 'Think what you like.'

His eyes were still on her face, and after a few moments he said quietly, 'I'm waiting for an answer.'

A man who proposed marriage was entitled to an answer. But she didn't feel ready to give it. She had been living from day to day, blocking out all thoughts of the end of their affair. She wasn't, she had been convinced, the sort of woman that a man like Gareth would think of marrying. She knew she had got herself into exactly the kind of situation she had meant to avoid, a drifting relationship leading nowhere, unless to certain heartache and disillusionment. But she had always been a fool about men, her only talent in that direction a penchant for choosing the wrong ones. This new development was totally unexpected and she ought to be over the moon, throwing herself into his arms in transports of gratitude. Only caution intervened. She wasn't at all sure of his motives.

'I don't know,' she said. 'It needs thinking about.'

His mouth thinned a little. 'Yes,' he said, 'I suppose it does. Let me know when you've decided, won't you?'

'I promise,' she said. 'You'll be the first to know.'

A faint, reluctant smile momentarily lit his eyes. His fingers encircled her throat in a mock threat as he bent to kiss her, his mouth a little impatient. 'I'll leave you to think about it,' he said and swung out of the bed to get his clothes.

Feeling oddly deserted, she watched him dress. He was tying his shoes when she said suddenly, 'Why do you want to marry me?'

He straightened, his smile derisive. 'Isn't it obvious?' he asked her dryly. His eyes swept the outline of her body under the sheet.

That's what I was afraid of, her mind said. It was the only thing they had in common, and she had travelled that road before and found it a dead end.

She watched him go, her eyes stormy and troubled. Long after the sound of the car had faded in the night she lay wakeful and restless, but in the morning she was no nearer to a decision.

Chapter Eight

She worked furiously for the next few days until the weekend, trying not to think of Gareth or of his proposal, and knowing that her attempt was futile. He didn't contact her and she was torn between relief and an odd resentment. Unable to stand her own company any longer, she phoned Claire quite early on Saturday and arranged to meet her for a look at a new shopping arcade in the city, and have lunch.

When they met, she saw why Pietro had been worried. Claire's waist was thickening and she wore a loose, pretty smock dress to hide it, but her legs were much too thin, her face looked pinched and under her eyes were transparent bluish patches. At first she was eager to explore the new shops, riffling through the racks of clothes in the boutiques, laughing ruefully as she admitted it wasn't much use her buying slim-fitting dresses, and leading Jess into a babywear and toy shop to demand her opinion of its wares.

But by lunchtime she had begun to flag, her steps dragging and her eyes growing dull with a fatigue she couldn't hide.

'Let's eat,' Jess said. 'You need to rest, don't you?'

'I'm all right.' But climbing the stairs to a restaurant on the mezzanine left her panting and she didn't protest as Jess found a table and made her sit down.

'Just get me a sandwich and some fruit juice, please, Jess,' she murmured, her head drooping.

'Shouldn't you have something more substantial?' Jess demanded when she returned with two sandwiches and the juice, plus her own plate and coffee.

'I'm not very hungry.' Claire took one of the sandwiches and looked at it with disfavour.

'Just now, or all the time?' Jess asked.

'I'm all right,' Claire reiterated.

'Pietro doesn't seem to think so.'

Claire said with some humour, 'Papa's worse than an old woman. Anyone would think I'm the only mother-to-be ever to suffer from a touch of morning sickness.'

'You look worn out. As though you had half a dozen little darlings to look after already.'

Claire smiled wanly. 'I don't know how mothers like that do cope with pregnancy. I must admit I feel dreadfully tired. But my doctor says it's very common.'

'You have mentioned it, then?'

'Yes, and he's given me some iron pills to take. I'll be perfectly fine in a month or two. Most afternoons I have a nap. Really, I'm shockingly spoiled. When I think of how the island women sail through their pregnancies and just keep on doing their normal household work it makes me feel ashamed.'

'Not everyone's the same. Is the sickness bad?'

'I should be getting over it soon. Please don't fuss, Jess. I have enough of that from Scott and Papa.' She paused. 'Have you seen Gareth lately?'

'You can take that innocent look off your face,' Jess said. 'Pietro told you, didn't he?'

Claire bit her lip, smiling. 'He did drop a hint. Is it serious, Jess?'

With an odd laugh, Jess said, 'Apparently it is. . . . He's asked me to marry him.'

Delight washed over Claire's face. 'Oh, that's great! I'm so glad for you.'

'I haven't said yes.'

'Oh,' Claire said doubtfully. 'Does that mean you're going to turn him down?'

Jess picked up a small cake off her plate, broke it in two and then dropped the halves back on the striped china. 'I probably should,' she said. 'We have nothing in common . . . and he doesn't really want a woman like me.'

'Scott and I didn't have much in common either,' Claire said, her eyes glowing, 'except that we loved each other. And what do you mean, Gareth doesn't want a woman like you? He wants *you,* or he wouldn't have asked you to marry him.'

'Denny wanted me, too,' Jess said bitterly, 'until I really needed him. By then the novelty had worn off.'

'Gareth isn't like that.'

'Gareth wouldn't ask for a divorce. But I don't want to wake up one morning and see him wondering why on earth he married me.'

'Why should he? Can't you trust in his love?'

'It isn't love,' Jess said bluntly. 'He isn't even pretending that it is.'

Claire flushed a little and looked at her consider-ingly. 'Are you sure?'

'Did you know he'd been engaged once?' Jess asked her.

'No. What happened?'

'She died. How do I compete with a memory? She was the kind of girl he should have married—gentle, good, sweet-natured.'

'Ugh, Jess!' Claire gurgled with laughter. 'I shouldn't think that would suit Gareth at all. He isn't a man for marshmallow!'

Jess stared for a moment. 'No, he's not, is he?' she said slowly.

'No.' Claire was positive. 'And you, Jess, are defi-nitely not marshmallow. Do you really think he's only asked you to marry him because he wants to get you into bed?'

Jess gave her friend a long, eloquent look. Claire flushed again, laughed and said, 'Sorry. That was silly of me, I suppose.'

'Have I shocked you?' Jess asked.

'Of course not. But . . . then why *do* you think he wants to marry you?'

'Exclusive rights.'

'Jealousy?' Claire shook her head. 'I don't think Gareth's like that. Not without . . . caring.'

'Would that make it love?' Jess asked cynically.

'Love has so many facets,' Claire mused. 'What about you, Jess? Is it love on your side?' With sudden insight she added softly, 'Is that why you're so hesitant about accepting him?'

She hadn't wanted to admit it, Jess realised. She had carefully avoided putting it into words, even to herself. Now Claire had brought the central issue starkly into the open and she had to face it. 'I think,' she said with deliberate lightness, 'that it must be. But you know me, Claire. I'm far too much of a coward ever to confess to it.'

'Not even to Gareth?'

'Especially not to him!' Jess said under her breath.

He phoned on Sunday, saying abruptly, 'I'm coming round. Will you be home?'

'Yes.' She quelled the impulse to make a smart answer. He didn't sound in the mood for it.

For the first time in weeks she violently craved a cigarette, and by the time he arrived she had worked herself into a simmering fever of nerves on the edge of temper.

She offered him a drink and he took it, but had only half finished it when he put his glass down on the table and said, 'I want an answer, Jess.'

She looked up at him over the rim of her glass and then lowered it to cradle it in her hands. 'I quite thought you'd begun to regret the question.'

He frowned, then gave an odd little laugh. 'Because I haven't been on the phone every day demanding a decision? I've had my hand on the receiver a dozen times and forced myself to wait. I've been giving you time, damn it!'

Carefully she placed her glass beside his. 'That,' she said, 'was very considerate of you.'

He waited a moment. 'Well? Or do you still,' he suggested sardonically, 'need more time?'

'No, I don't need any more time. I accept.'

He said, very formally, 'Thank you.' He didn't move, and she was looking at her tightly clasped hands, not at his face. She stood up and he followed suit, and, almost on a level with him, she met his unsmiling eyes.

She said, 'There's a condition.'

'I had the feeling that there might be.' His voice was soft, but his mouth looked rather unpleasantly grim.

'I want a three months' engagement,' Jess said. 'And no sex until the wedding.'

Surprise wrung a small, amazed laugh from him. *'Why?'*

Giving a tiny shrug, she glanced again at her hands, then looked at him sideways and murmured, 'Would you believe . . . moral scruples?'

He frowned and said curtly, 'No, I wouldn't. What are you playing at, Jess?'

'I'm not playing. Marriage is . . . hopefully . . . for keeps, isn't it?'

'I certainly intend it to be. You won't get out of this one easily.'

She turned away and he said quickly, 'I didn't mean to be brutal, but you might as well know. I *am* playing for keeps.'

Yes, he would be. Not for him the scandal and humiliation of a divorce. 'Well then,' she said, 'all the more reason to be sure.'

'Sure of what?'

'That we know what we're doing. An engagement is supposed to be a sort of trial period, isn't it? To make certain we're compatible . . . that kind of thing.'

'I'd have thought we'd already done that, fairly thoroughly.'

She turned on him. *'No,* that's just it! We jumped into bed before we were even sure we *liked* each other! Until that night we . . . Well, I'm not sure if we have anything else but compatibility in bed. It was all too . . . too quick.'

'At least it got some of the barriers out of the way.'

'Is that what you intended?'

'I didn't cold-bloodedly plan a seduction, if that's what you mean. And I wasn't unsure about liking you.'

'No?'

'No,' he said positively. 'Are *you* in the habit of going to bed with people you dislike?'

Jess flushed and made a defeated little gesture, shaking her head.

'Am I to suppose you made an exception in my case?' he asked dryly.

'You know it wasn't like that,' she said, her voice low.

'No, it wasn't, was it?' He put out his hand and touched her cheek with his long, strong fingers, and his expression softened into a half smile. 'Jess,' he said, 'why don't you let down your guard and trust me?'

He was very near to understanding her, and she desperately wanted to do as he asked. But past hurts and betrayals intervened . . . and the fact that she was uncertain of what he actually felt for her. She closed her eyes against the insistence of his and said unsteadily, 'Please, Gareth . . . give me time.'

He gave a sharp sigh and the caressing hand fell away. 'All right,' he said, 'if that's what you want. But I'm going to put a ring on your finger and I won't take no for an answer on that!'

Perhaps because she had so nearly capitulated, she snapped back with, 'Are you sure you don't want to put it through my nose?'

He laughed and shook his head. 'You've got the

wrong idea, darling. I don't want to subjugate you . . . even if I thought I could.'

He had never called her that before, and the endearment had the strangest effect on her; she had a swift and fleeting desire to fall at his feet and kiss his hands, to give him the submission he had not asked for and never would. Shocked at such a bizarre impulse, she swallowed and on a quick breath said, 'You don't want to give me a diamond, do you? I'm not fond of them.'

'No diamond then,' he agreed easily. 'What about an opal? Are you superstitious?'

'It's my birthstone,' she said, 'so opals aren't bad luck for me.'

'Right, then. We'll look for an opal.' He took her left hand lightly in his and spread her fingers on his palm. 'You've got good hands for rings; I've often thought you should wear one.' He touched the third finger. 'An oval shape, I think . . . something dark and fiery.'

She hadn't worn a ring since removing Denny's wedding band. 'Rings are very constricting,' she said.

He looked at her, knowing what she meant. 'They don't need to be.'

'But sometimes,' she said, 'they slip off too easily.'

'Mine,' he said, 'will stay put. But I promise it won't be constricting.'

It was a beautiful solid opal—almost black, and shot with green, amber and gold. Two tiny emeralds flanked the central cabochon on a hoop of gold. He slid it onto her finger one evening at his apartment, regarded it with satisfaction for a moment or two, then lifted her hand to his lips and turned her palm to his mouth.

She felt the warm flick of his tongue in the hollow of her hand and bit her lip, her breath quickening. Gareth looked up and pulled her into his arms, kissing her eyelids, her mouth, her throat. Instinctively her body curved into his, her hand sliding to his shoulders. His arm about her waist drew her closer, and one hand rested possessively on her breast.

He raised his head and she offered him her mouth, catching a glimpse of his eyes, fever-bright between narrowed lids, before she gave herself up to the erotic persuasion of his kiss.

When his mouth left hers he brought his lips to the smooth skin of her shoulder. 'Do you really mean to stick to that condition you made?' he asked with a thread of amusement.

Almost unbearably tempted, Jess was silent for a moment. But the hint of laughter in his voice helped to put her on her mettle. He so obviously thought she wouldn't stand by her decision.

'Yes,' she said at last, easing herself away from him.

He let her move only an inch or two, then held her, his hands firm on her waist. 'Sure?' he enquired, his smile coaxing, his eyes brilliant with desire.

'Please, Gareth,' she said breathlessly.

He regarded her a moment longer before his hands reluctantly fell away. 'It's going to take a lot of will-power,'' he said.

'Do you intend to make it hard for me?'

'I meant on both sides,' he told her.

She regarded him uncertainly. Vaguely she had felt that he thought the limits she had set on their engagement were just a whim, one that he needn't take too seriously.

'What's the matter?' His smile was speculative. 'Regretting your terms, Jess?'

'No.' She shook her head. It might be difficult, but she felt they needed this respite from the winds of passion that had swirled about them for weeks. Men, even those as civilised and intelligent as Gareth, were apt to put sex at the top of the compatibility index. Women demanded more, and Jess was no exception.

She was nervous about meeting Gareth's parents again, wearing his ring, but of course it had to be faced. They were invited for Sunday lunch the weekend after her acceptance, and she dressed with great care in a cream linen skirt with big pockets in which she could hide her shaking hands, and an amber silk shirt with a rope of seed pearls. She hoped she looked suitable to be received into one of Sydney's oldest families.

Gareth seemed to approve, anyway, if the faint glow in his eyes when he surveyed her as they walked to his car was any indication. He looked good, too, she thought dispassionately, in charcoal slacks and a deep red open-necked shirt.

'You must learn to drive, Jess,' he said as he started the car. 'I can give you a lesson after lunch if you like.'

'No, thanks.'

He glanced at her curiously. 'Don't you trust me?'

'I just don't want to drive.' She turned to gaze at the view from the side window.

'Have you ever tried?'

'A long time ago.'

'And?'

'And nothing. I manage quite adequately without a license, thank you. Now, can we please drop the subject?'

'Did you have an accident or something?' he asked.

Gritting her teeth, Jess said, 'You could say that.'

For some minutes he drove in silence. Then he said quietly, 'Jess, if this engagement period is supposed to help us get to know each other better, it isn't going to work too well if you freeze up every time I ask about some apparently traumatic event in your past. It must have given you quite a shakeup if it stopped you from ever wanting to drive again.'

'I wasn't driving at the time,' she said. 'Denny was. Do you want to hear all about my married life?'

'No,' he said, 'but I'm not such a fool that I think we can pretend it never happened. You don't have to keep a clamp on everything you and Denny did together.'

She said, 'He was driving; we had an accident. I was in the hospital for weeks. It's over, and I don't want to think about it. I had been learning to drive before that. Afterwards I just lost any desire to continue my lessons.'

She had lost any desire to do anything much after the accident, but she didn't want to tell him about that. For months after leaving the hospital, it had taken all her willpower just to sit in a car as a passenger, and the thought of driving herself had made her literally shake with fear.

She clenched her fists on her lap, swept suddenly by another memory which she had tried to suppress. A cold dew of sweat gathered on her temples. 'Gareth . . .'

He shot a swift look at her and drew the car onto the roadside, turning to take her hands in his. 'Jess,' he said, 'I didn't mean to nag, or upset you.' His hands chafed hers, easing the clenched fingers open. 'Are you all right?'

'Yes.' But she had to tell him. . . .

'Here,' he said. 'Lean on me, darling.' He drew her into his arms and brought her forehead down against his shirt, massaging the back of her neck, and Jess fought a weak desire to cry. His fingers were soothing and the warmth of his body through the shirt was comforting against her cheek. She sighed, wanting to lie there for a little while before she unburdened the confession that she must make.

But when she stirred, lifting her head, her lips parting on the words, he closed them with his in a long, soft, utterly blissful kiss, and his expression when he held her away from him was so tender, his voice so concerned as he murmured, 'Better?' that she couldn't bear to shatter the moment. She nodded, smiling, and he put her back against the seat, dropped a kiss on her forehead and said, 'We'd better get on. They'll have only too good an idea of what we're doing.'

She busied herself renewing her tawny lip gloss as he drove, and trying to steady her leaping pulses. Her conscience nagged at her dimly, and she promised it, I will tell him, I will . . . but not just now.

Mrs. Seymour welcomed her with a kiss and called her 'dear,' surprising Jess considerably. In spite of that, Jess had the impression that she was determined to make the best of a state of affairs that she thought rather a pity.

Gareth's parents had made a small family gathering of it. His sister and her husband had flown from Perth specially to meet Jess, apparently. Perhaps, Jess thought unfairly, Mrs. Seymour had felt that she needed reinforcements.

Fiona was like her mother to look at, but less aloof, and Craig Hogarth was a handsome, thickset man with a gentle manner and a quiet wit. Jess was pleased to find that she liked them and that they seemed to like her, too. There was an air of relief in Fiona's congratulations and in her husband's hearty handshake that led Jess to tease Gareth later.

'Had they given up hope of you?' she asked him, with a sidelong glance. 'They seem very glad to see you roped and tied at last.'

They were strolling in the garden that overlooked a bend in the river, Gareth's arm about her shoulders, her hands in the deep side pockets of her skirt.

'Have you roped and tied me?' he asked her, his eyes gleaming down at her face. 'If so, it's mutual, surely?'

'I don't know, actually,' she said, almost seriously. 'My researches into convict women have led me into some odd byways lately.'

'Such as?' he asked curiously.

'Feminist theory, for one thing. Remember when I told you that the women in the eighteenth and nineteenth centuries had to get some man to back them when they wanted to do anything with their lives?'

'Yes.'

'Well, in some ways things haven't changed all that much. The world, so the feminist writers think, is still organised around male values, and men still expect to run it.'

Mildly he said, 'Is this relevant to our relationship? I don't think I'm a male chauvinist. I've certainly tried not to be.'

'Have you?' It was her turn to give him a curious look.

'Am I so unsuccessful?' he asked.

Jess laughed. 'No, not really. There are times, though, when you like to . . . dominate.'

'If you're talking about lovemaking,' he said, 'there are times when *you* like to be dominated—in spite of your independent spirit. That sort of thing is no more than a private and intimate game. You know I'd never force you if you really weren't willing.'

'Wouldn't you?' She stopped walking to look at him directly.

Faint shock showed in his eyes. Almost angrily, he said, 'No! I'm not a savage. And I happen to like women, in general. I don't get any kick out of humiliating them.'

She started to walk on, saying, 'Marriage, according to one school of thought, is merely a way for males to assert ownership over females and—and their offspring.'

'Legitimate heirs and all that,' he said, amused. 'I can read, too.'

They had stopped at the river bank; Jess took a dead brown twig from an overhanging red gum and tossed it into the water, watching it swirl and hesitate before being borne away on the current. 'There's something you should know if you're going to marry me,' she said, hating the sound of her own voice, careless and insouciant. 'No legitimate heirs, I'm afraid. I can't have children.'

She remained staring at the water, the dark eddies and sun-gilded ripples that ruffled its smooth surface. Her hands were back again in the enveloping pockets; her fingers curled into her damp palms until the nails stung her flesh. Gareth stood unmoving beside her, and she felt the hard, incredulous rake of his eyes on her profile as she delivered the throwaway line that must have shocked him to the core.

At last he said, 'Thank you for telling me.'

Jess turned then, swiftly, her eyes questioning, anxious in spite of herself. 'You had a right to know,' she said. 'You can have your ring back if you like. I won't hold it against you.'

Her hands came out of her pockets, and she touched the opal ring, ready to offer it to him. But he quickly stopped her, his fingers encircling her wrist.

'I don't want it back,' he said gently.

'Aren't you disappointed not to be able to plan a family?'

He hesitated, then said, 'Yes, a little. But I'll get used to the idea, and it isn't that important. If we feel the lack too keenly, there's always the chance of adoption.'

'It's not the same, is it?'

'I don't suppose it is. That doesn't mean it can't be just as good, though. I know several couples with very happy adopted families. It's something we can think about, anyway.'

'If you change your mind . . .' she said jerkily.

'I am not going to change my mind,' he told her, his hands gripping her arms. 'As you said a while ago, it's taken me long enough, in my family's estimation, to make it up in the first place. Come here, woman, and kiss me!'

'Dominant,' she murmured, regarding him with gleaming half-closed eyes. 'Male chauvinist p—'

The rest was lost in his mouth as it descended on hers. Fierce with relief, she responded with her arms locked about his neck, until he pulled away and looked down at her. 'You were saying?'

'I don't remember,' she said innocently.

He grunted, and one hand went to her blouse, opening the buttons, ignoring her faint protest. He guided her round to the other side of the red gum so that they were hidden from the river, and screened from the house by a group of scarlet bottlebrushes in full flower. 'It's almost a public place,' he told her. 'You're perfectly safe from ravishment, unfortunately.'

Laughing inwardly, she said in pretended alarm, 'I wouldn't count on it!' And he trapped her against the pale, stained bark with his thighs, his hands on her breasts, his lips exploring her throat, until she sighed shudderingly and sagged against him, held up only by his strength and the clutch of her hands on his shoulders.

'Oh, don't, don't!' she begged him, her eyes closed, her voice a hoarse whisper.

His mouth was hot against the curve of flesh thrusting from her opened blouse. He lifted dazed eyes and said, 'You drive me crazy and you know it, don't you?'

Gasping, she said, 'You're not on your own!'

He laughed unsteadily and moved with breathtaking suddenness, hooking his arm about her waist so that he leaned on the tree, holding her yielding body to him. He wrapped his other arm about her and hugged her closely, and she felt him taking deep breaths, striving for control. She burrowed her head into the open neck of his shirt and resisted the wild urge to open her mouth against his skin, turning her cheek to it instead, and waiting, waiting for the fire to recede.

When her blood was racing less wildly, she wriggled out of his embrace and did up her blouse. He watched intently, arms folded across his chest, and she thought his mouth held a tinge of satisfaction because her trembling fingers had difficulty getting the buttons through the holes.

'We'd better be getting back to the house, hadn't we?' she said, amazed that her voice sounded normal.

'I suppose so,' he said, 'much as I'd like to spend the afternoon making love to you.'

Fiona and Craig had gone to have a game of tennis on the lawn court at the back of the house; Mrs. Seymour's plans for the afternoon, to the amusement of her husband, who retired behind a Sunday newspaper, included showing Jess a collection of family albums—not just photographs of Gareth and Fiona as children, but older portraits dating back to the first Seymours who had lived in the house. 'Five generations of them now. And when his father and I are gone, Gareth—and you, of course, Jess—will bring your children to live here, I hope.'

Jess looked up at Gareth, sitting opposite while his mother and she were on the sofa, an album on Jess's knee.

'Don't count your chickens, Mother,' he said easily. 'Children may not figure in our plans.'

'Not figure . . . ?' Mrs. Seymour looked astounded. 'But surely . . .'

Jess said, 'I can't have children, Mrs. Seymour.' Thank God she had told Gareth, she thought.

If he had been anything like as shocked as his mother looked, he had hidden it well. Mrs. Seymour seemed to have aged ten years in an instant, her face greyish except for two high spots of colour on her aristocratic cheekbones. 'Gareth!' she said to her son. 'How *could* you!'

'It isn't important, Mother,' Gareth said sharply.

'But, Gareth, of *course* it's . . .' Her anguished voice was rising, and her husband looked up from his paper and said, 'Julia . . .'

She stopped abruptly, with a visible effort. Turning

to Jess, she said stiffly, 'My dear, I'm so sorry. That was unforgivable of me. I'm afraid I've taken it for granted. . . . You see, there have always been Seymours at Karunja. I hoped . . . but if Gareth says it doesn't matter'—she smiled bravely—'then, of course, it doesn't. Now, here is Gareth's great-great-grandmother. A formidable lady, don't you think? Though actually they all tended to look rather grim, from having to sit perfectly still while the early photographers took their pictures. . . .'

As Gareth drove her home Jess said, 'Your mother is horrified, you realise that?'

'She'll get over it. It's just that she has this strong feeling for family tradition. I've never found it so vital, myself.'

'Gareth, if you're being chivalrous . . .'

His laugh was natural enough. 'Forget it, Jess. Mother will recover from her disappointment, and Fiona may fill the gap eventually. She and Craig plan to have a family. Maybe it's time there was a change from Seymours at Karunja, anyway.'

'I have a strong feeling that your mother would think that was heresy.'

He grinned. 'Probably. Considering she married into the Seymours herself, she's remarkably steeped in the family lore. She's the one to talk to about history, really.'

'What about her own family?'

'English immigrant clergy in the late nineteenth century . . . younger sons of the squirarchy. My forbears were a very dull lot. By the way, have you told your parents about our engagement?'

'Not yet,' Jess answered cautiously. 'I told you they live in Brisbane.'

'There are such things as telephones and mail services,' he reminded her.

'Yes, I've heard of them,' she said. 'Whatever will they think of next?'

He shot her a laughingly exasperated glance and said no more on the subject.

Chapter Nine

*E*ventually she brought herself to write to her mother that she was planning to be married again. By return post came a large, gold-embossed card of congratulation, and an anxious letter hoping that she was sure she knew what she was doing and giving guarded thanks that at least this time it couldn't be because she was pregnant.

Jess tore up the letter, but at the last moment rescued the card from the rubbish bin and displayed it for Gareth's benefit on the mantelpiece. Other cards arrived, including one from Claire and Scott expressing their best and loving wishes, and she put them alongside her mother's. She phoned Claire to thank her and to ask how she was, and was somewhat reassured by the cheerfulness of her friend's voice and the liveliness of her conversation, which was still largely about the coming baby and the preparations being made for it.

Pietro had received their news with what seemed to Gareth to be surprising enthusiasm. He insisted on throwing a party for them and, to Jess's considerable amusement, appeared to consider himself almost wholly responsible for the engagement.

The day of the party Jess put the cover on her typewriter earlier than usual, had a long shower and washed her hair. She was pulling on a short cotton housecoat when the doorbell rang. Hastily she wrapped a towel about her head and padded barefoot to the door.

'Hello, Jess,' Scott said, his blue glance faintly humorous as he took in her attire, but he had a strained look about his eyes. 'May I come in?'

'Yes, of course.' Jess stood aside. 'Make yourself at home while I do something with my hair, will you?'

After she had rough-dried it and combed the damp curls into shape, she went to join Scott. He was still standing, looking as though he might have been pacing the room while he waited.

'Is everything all right, Scott?'

'Not so you'd notice,' he said rather shortly.

Curious, she asked, 'What's the trouble? Have you and Claire quarrelled?'

He shot her a glance and said, 'You could say that.'

'Look, Scott,' she said carefully, 'I won't be your wailing wall if you two have fallen out. Why don't you go back to her and—'

'It isn't like that!' he interrupted impatiently. 'It's far more serious than a marital spat, Jess. Claire's life may be at stake.'

Staring, she said, 'What?'

Thrusting a hand through his hair, he stood frowning

in the middle of the room. Jerkily he said, 'I know she'll hate it if she finds out I've told you. She doesn't want anyone to know. But I thought you might talk to her. If you could just get her to see sense . . .'

Disturbed by the anguished pleading in his face, Jess said, 'Hang on, Scott. Sit down and I'll pour us both a drink.'

'I could certainly do with one,' he said.

Glancing at him worriedly, Jess swiftly poured two stiff whiskies. Handing one to him, she gestured to the sofa, and at last he obeyed, subsiding on the upholstered seat with his shoulders hunched, his drink held between his hands.

Jess perched on the arm and said quietly, 'Now, what's it all about, Scott?'

'She has a heart condition.' He gulped at the drink. 'Stenosis of the aortic valve, they call it. Do you want to hear all the medical details?'

'They wouldn't mean much to me,' Jess said, shaking her head as a wave of shock hit her. 'Did she know when you started the baby?'

'No. We found out a couple of days ago.'

'But surely she must have had some inkling?'

'None, she says, bar a bit of dizziness and breathlessness now and then, which she put down to various minor causes at the time. The valve must have narrowed quite a while ago, apparently it's often traceable to rheumatic fever in childhood and she doesn't know about that. . . . She remembers being sick a couple of times before her mother left her at the orphanage, but she doesn't know what she had. And it's quite usual for the heart to compensate by pumping more strongly so that people can go on into middle age without knowing they have this "incompetent" valve. Anyway, there were no real symptoms until the pregnancy created an extra strain on her heart.'

'Shouldn't her doctor have picked it up before now? What's he been doing?'

'Putting it all down to morning sickness and the vagaries of pregnancy,' Scott said grimly. 'He says he did detect a slight irregularity of the heart when he first examined her, what used to be called a "murmur," but that's not uncommon, and according to him it's often found in quite healthy people, so he did nothing.'

'She ought to change her doctor!' Jess suggested forcefully.

'Yes, well, that's one of the problems.'

'You mean medical ethics or something?'

'No, it's not that. I was worried about her; she seemed so thin and tired. Then the other night she had a fit of breathlessness in bed. No'—he gave the ghost of a grin at her raised brows—'we weren't making love; she was resting. I spoke to the doctor about it, though she didn't want me to, and insisted on him investigating thoroughly. He did some tests, and now he wants another opinion on her condition in relation to the pregnancy.' He paused. 'I shouldn't be burdening you with this on the night of your engagement party, I know, but I'm desperate. And there may not be much time. Claire won't see the specialist Dr. Barton recommended. I hoped you might be able to make an opportunity to see her alone and get her to confide in you. If you could only persuade her to see this man . . .'

Not understanding, Jess began to say, 'But why won't she . . . ?' Then, sudden light dawning, she said instead, 'What kind of specialist, Scott?'

He avoided her eyes. 'It's possible . . . that she should have an abortion. The doctor thinks it may be necessary . . . that's why he wants another opinion.'

'But Claire would never accept that!'

'She *must* accept it, Jess, if it's going to save her life!'

Jess looked at distress and frustration in his face and sighed hopelessly. 'I can't help you, Scott. I can't make her do something she doesn't want to. . . .'

'Jess, she might *die!*' He dropped his head on one hand suddenly and his shoulders heaved as he took a deep, steadying breath. 'Please, Jess,' he said, looking up, his eyes dry but filled with pain, 'try and talk to her. I can't, anymore. She isn't listening to me.'

'What about Pietro?'

'She made me promise at the start not to tell him. I shouldn't have. We were both pretty upset at the time and I thought I'd be able to talk her round on my own.' He shook his head. 'I can't. But she might listen to you . . . another woman, and one she's fond of. Look, I want this baby, too, but not at the cost of Claire's life—or health. If she'd only see this man . . . It may not be as bad as Dr. Barton thinks. She says there's no point because whatever happens she's going ahead with the pregnancy. She won't see reason at all.'

Jess regarded him thoughtfully. 'Maybe her idea of reason is different from yours.'

'Oh, for God's sake! Surely you're not on her side?'

'Do I have to take sides?' Jess asked quietly.

For a moment he put a hand to his face again. 'No, of course not.' He sighed. 'But for the first time since we've been married, Claire and I are on opposite sides of some high, impregnable fence. I can't get through to her, Jess. Someone has to persuade her to see this doctor. I guess I'm going about it the wrong way. Only

I'm so . . . so frightened. All I can think of is that she *has* to live. Nothing matters but that.'

'And supposing this specialist *does* recommend an abortion, Scott? What then?'

He said in a low voice, 'Then I'll have to make sure that she has it.'

She looked at the gaunt determination in his face and warned, 'She may hate you for it. Has that occurred to you?'

He flinched and looked away. 'If that happens,' he said, 'I'll just have to live with it. At least she'll be alive. What I couldn't live with is knowing that I let her die.'

'Scott, I—'

She was interrupted by the ringing of the doorbell. 'Sorry,' she said. 'Excuse me.'

She was just into the narrow passageway when he came after her to catch at her hand. 'Jess . . . don't say anything about this to anyone, will you? And when you speak to Claire, try and make her tell you about it without mentioning that I've already talked to you . . . please?'

She hesitated. 'Yes, all right, I promise.'

Instead of freeing her hand he lifted it to his lips and dropped a quick kiss of gratitude on her fingers, just as the key turned in the lock and Gareth stepped into the hall.

His sudden, sharp stillness was noticeable before he closed the door carefully behind him and said to Jess, 'I thought you must be out—or in the shower.' She had given him a key, but he always scrupulously rang before letting himself in.

Taking her hand from Scott's loosened grasp, she said calmly, 'I was when Scott arrived. You're early.'

He glanced at the gold watch on his wrist. 'Hardly. I did say I'd be here at six thirty.'

'Is that the time?' Her eyes widened.

'Yes, actually. Time flies when you're having fun, doesn't it?' he said pleasantly. 'How are you, Scott?'

'Okay,' Scott answered tersely. 'Sorry, Jess, it's your big night and I didn't mean to . . . keep you talking. Forgive me.'

'Of course,' she assured him. 'Gareth, why don't you get yourself a drink while I see Scott out?'

Gareth, unsmiling and silent, went past them into the sitting room, and she opened the door for Scott.

'If Gareth mentions I've seen you tonight . . .' Scott murmured, looking harassed.

Jess touched his hand. 'I'll deal with Gareth. And I'll try to get Claire to talk to me. More than that I can't promise.'

'Bless you,' he said, and gave her a brief hug before starting down the steps.

Jess returned slowly to the sitting room.

Gareth was standing by the sideboard, a drink in his hand. 'Want one?' he asked.

'No, thanks,' she said. 'I had one with Scott.'

Their eyes held. Jess said, 'I'd like you not to mention to Claire—or anyone—tonight that Scott was here.'

His brows rose a tiny fraction. 'May one ask why?' he asked, his words clipped and precise.

'I can't tell you,' she admitted, adding quickly, 'Please trust me, Gareth.'

He studied her in silence. Then something in his face changed, an indefinable expression flitting across it, leaving his steady gaze fractionally less icy. 'I trust you, Jess,' he said quietly.

Relief filled her. Her taut body relaxed and without thought she swiftly crossed the room to him. He put down his drink and drew her into his arms as she reached him, resting her head on his shoulder to say against his coat, 'Thank you, Gareth.'

His arms tightened and he kissed her cheek and the corner of her mouth, teasing at it with his tongue until she lifted her face and let him kiss her fully on the mouth. Ardently she returned the pressure of his lips, and with subtle movements incited the hands that ran over her body. When one intruded inside her robe, she felt a fierce response and made a small sound against his mouth but then drew back, flushed and tousled. 'We'll be late,' she said.

'Yes,' he agreed gravely. 'And, besides, it isn't in our bargain, is it?'

'I don't remember talking of bargains. It was a simple request, that's all.'

'Condition, you said.'

She had, too, she remembered. 'Anyway, we can't argue now. I'll go and get dressed.' But his straying hand was still at her collar, and he slid his fingers under the cotton and widened the front opening, almost baring her breasts.

'Can I watch?' he said softly.

'No!' She pushed him away and folded the gown about her. He might be able to stand it, but she was very sure she wouldn't be able to bear having his caressing eyes on her as she changed without throwing herself into his arms and forgetting the party, the 'condition' she had made, and the entire world, for a few heady minutes of his lovemaking.

* * *

Vivienne Tapper was looking particularly attractive in a chiffon dress with a floating skirt that stopped at the knee and showed off her pretty legs. Claire's two teenage half-brothers added a lively young note to the party, and Sheryl and Morris Quinn, newly returned from their honeymoon, brought with them a strong aura of married bliss.

Scott and Claire arrived late, Scott carrying a large, gift-wrapped parcel. Jess was glad to see that there was some colour in Claire's cheeks, but a closer glimpse made her wonder if it was due to skilfully applied blusher, because the rest of her skin was translucently pale. Trying not to show her anxiety, she took the parcel Scott handed over and unwrapped an antique-framed watercolour of Old Sydney Harbour, dated 1863.

'Oh, it's gorgeous!' she exclaimed with genuine pleasure. 'How did you find it?'

'Sheer luck,' Scott told her. 'We knew you'd like it, didn't we, darling?'

Claire's smile was tight and she kept her eyes fastened on the picture. 'I don't know if it's the period you're researching for your book,' she said, 'but I hope you both will enjoy having it in your home. Have you decided yet where you're going to live?'

Jess shook her head, and Gareth said, 'We still have to discuss minor matters like that.'

Laughter greeted his remark, and Pietro said, 'Can I get you a drink, Scott? Claire—a lemonade, perhaps, for you?'

Jess got very little chance during the first part of the evening to speak to Claire, but managed to say to

Scott when he offered to refill her glass, 'How are things?'

'Hellish,' he returned under his breath. 'Look at her. She's keeping going on nothing but nervous energy and sheer stubborn will.'

Claire was sitting with Jonnie, the older of her half-brothers, trying an inexpert version of 'Chopsticks' with him on the piano and giggling at their mistakes.

Later someone put on tapes of dance music, and Gareth took Jess in his arms as some of the others began to dance in a cleared corner of the room. 'Nice party,' he said.

'Yes.'

'Do you know what's the matter with Claire?'

Her eyes flickered away. 'She's pregnant.'

'She's unhappy.'

So he had noticed. He might have resigned himself to Claire's belonging to Scott, he might want to make love to Jess herself so badly that at times she felt his frustration as a physical ache in her own being, but he still picked up emanations from Claire, knew when she was unhappy.

Rather tartly, Jess said, 'She's not the only one.'

'Scott?' Gareth glanced over to where Scott stood with his father-in-law. 'Have they quarrelled?'

She gave him a long stare and said evenly, 'How would I know?'

'Yes,' he said slowly, staring right back. 'How, indeed?'

The tempo of the music became faster, and Jess saw Jonnie laughingly drag Claire onto the floor. Scott turned as if to protest, but Jonnie held Claire carefully, grinned at his brother-in-law and said something that must have reassured him. Scott returned to stand again by Pietro.

When the music stopped Claire, breathless but laughing, was being escorted back to her husband by her half-brother when her face went paper-white and she sagged at the knees.

Scott was there even before Jonnie, his handsome young face filled with bewildered alarm, had realised what was happening. Scooping his wife into his arms, Scott lifted her easily, barking to Pietro, 'Get a doctor!'

'No!' Claire's voice was high and clear. 'No, Papa. I'm just a little dizzy, that's all.'

'Get one!' Scott reiterated harshly as Claire began to struggle weakly in his arms. He strode out of the room in the direction of Claire's old bedroom. Vivienne said worriedly, 'Can I help at all?' only to be ignored. Jess slipped after Scott, and reached the bedroom in time to hear him say in a low, shaking voice, 'Lie still or so help me I'll *make* you!'

'I shouldn't think that would do anyone much good,' Jess said crisply.

Scott turned a furious look on her, and she warned him with a glance.

'Jess!' Claire panted, struggling into a sitting position and leaning against the headboard. 'I'm so sorry; I'm spoiling your party, and there's no need. I'll be fine in a few minutes. Don't let Papa drag a doctor out for me.' There was a cold, blue look about her lips, though her cheeks had regained their overbright colour.

'I think he's already on the phone,' Jess said. 'And don't you think it would be best to have a doctor make sure you're okay?'

'I *am* okay,' Claire said. 'Just a bit of faintness . . .'

Scott interrupted harshly, 'Jess knows.'

Jess cast him a humorous glance. He had, after all, sworn her to secrecy.

'Knows what?' Claire asked sharply. 'That you want me to have an abortion?'

'I don't *want* you to have an abortion!' Scott almost shouted. 'I want you to *live.*'

'Scott,' Jess said, 'why don't you go and see if Pietro's got a doctor yet?'

Understanding perfectly, he gave her a tight-lipped look and said, 'Yes, okay. Look after her, Jess.'

When he had gone, she propped a pillow behind Claire, sat on the side of the bed and said, 'Want to tell me about it?'

'Why? Scott's already done that, hasn't he?' Claire asked wearily.

'His version,' Jess agreed. 'He loves you.'

Claire looked as though she was about to disagree. Then her pinched mouth wavered, and she turned her head aside. Jess could see a vein throbbing faintly in her neck. 'I know. That's why it's so hard . . .'

'To hold out against him?' Jess asked shrewdly.

Claire nodded miserably. 'He doesn't understand. I can't just get rid of this baby. I can't even think about it.'

'He's only asked you to see a specialist, hasn't he?'

Gritting her teeth, Claire said, 'I won't . . .' Tears rolled down her cheeks.

'You're afraid that he'll suggest an abortion?'

Claire nodded.

'It doesn't seem sensible to flatly refuse to seek a second opinion,' Jess said diffidently.

'I am not going to . . .'

'Look, he might decide there's no need for it. And in any case, no one can force you to do it.'

Claire looked at her almost suspiciously, then said, as though it was a new idea, 'Yes. I suppose you're right. But Scott would try.' She put a hand to her temple and said, 'I'm afraid my thinking has become fairly muddled. It's all rather . . . horrible. You'd think a thing like this would bring us closer, wouldn't you? But it seems to be driving a wedge a mile wide between us instead.'

'Scott said you were on opposite sides of some impregnable barrier.'

Claire almost smiled, but her eyes were sad. 'Yes. I wouldn't have thought it could happen to us. There's been so much love. But Scott isn't used to being thwarted. He doesn't know how to cope with that except to try and bully me into doing what he wants.'

'He wants what's best for you,' Jess protested mildly.

'He wants what *he* thinks is best for me,' Claire argued. 'What he's been advised is best, admittedly. But it isn't quite the same thing. When the doctor told us what he'd found, I barely had time to recover from the initial shock before he said "termination" might be indicated. I said, "No!" And Scott, without even a glance in my direction, just said quite calmly, "If that's necessary, then of course she'll have it." I was sick with—I don't know—fear and . . . disappointment, I suppose. It was as though he had betrayed me. He didn't seem to take into account how I felt about it at all. The doctor gave him the specialist's address and a note for him, and Scott took them and said we'd go and see him as soon as we could get an appointment. The two of them sat there and *they* decided what was best for me, and I had this nightmare vision of the other doctor doing the same thing, of him and Scott deciding to destroy our baby without even asking for my opinion.'

'It might not come to that,' Jess told her.

'That isn't really the point. What shattered me was Scott's attitude. As though *my* feelings about the whole thing were irrelevant. What I wanted didn't seem to *matter!*'

'He's terrified of losing you,' Jess said. 'And he doesn't share your faith, you know that.'

'Yes, when I married him I knew I was taking a leap in the dark. He was perfectly open-minded about it; he was even willing to go along with . . . with my beliefs about birth control. But now . . . he thinks I'm being blindly obedient to some cruel, arbitrary law. And it isn't like that. I've felt my child moving within me. I can't kill it. I couldn't live with the guilt . . . the grief.'

'Scott said he couldn't live with the knowledge that he'd let you die.'

Claire bit her lip, and her eyes filled with tears. 'There are worse things,' she said, 'than dying.'

Pietro came in, tapping softly first on the door. 'My own doctor is on his way,' he said, coming over to the bed. 'Scott spoke to him and explained that it is necessary. Why didn't you tell me, Claire? Surely I had a right to know about these complications?'

'It's been . . . difficult,' Claire said. 'I'm sorry, Papa. And sorry to have spoiled your party. I feel fine now, and I'm sure it isn't necessary to call out any doctor.'

'He is on his way,' Pietro said.

Claire looked slightly more relaxed. 'I'm sure I don't need him,' she repeated. 'Jess, please go back to the party. You, too, Papa.'

'No, I'll keep you company for a little while,' Pietro said. 'Jess, go and tell Scott that Claire feels better, hmm?'

Scott was waiting by the phone with one eye on the front door of the apartment. He swung his head quickly in Jess's direction as she approached, and she answered the question in his eyes first. 'She's better. Much better. And Scott,' she added as she came close to him, 'I think she's willing to see a specialist.'

He closed his eyes tightly and seemed to sway with relief so that she put a hand quickly on his arm. He gripped her shoulders hard, his face on her hair. 'Thank God!' he breathed. 'Oh, Jess, you're a wonder!'

She put her hand to his hair in a quick gesture of understanding and comfort. 'Yes, aren't I?' she said, gently easing away from him.

'She won't entertain the idea of abortion, though,' Jess warned. Seeing his face take on a stubborn look, she urged, 'Try and see her point of view.'

'Do you think I haven't?' he asked her fiercely.

'I think you're having great difficulty,' she answered, not without compassion. 'For you the worst thing that can happen to her is for her to die. Claire thinks differently. She believes in eternity.'

'But I don't!' he said. 'I can't!'

The doorbell pealed and Scott almost leaped to answer it. As the doctor entered the hall, Jess went to join the other rather subdued guests.

'How is she?' Gareth asked for all of them.

'Feeling much better, and the doctor's just come.' Vivienne was handing round cups of coffee and Jess took one gratefully. 'She's very embarrassed, though.'

'She seemed fine when we were dancing,' Jonnie said. 'She was laughing. It wasn't until we stopped . . .'

One of the women said practically, 'She'll be all right. Scott's probably just fussing. Men tend to do that with a first pregnancy.' She sent a sly glance in her husband's direction. Sheryl giggled and said coyly to Morris, 'Will you panic like that when I get pregnant and throw a fainting fit, Morrie?'

Morris slapped her bottom and growled some comment, and she squealed delightedly. Sheryl, Jess reflected, had never heard of feminism, or if she had, she was willing to ignore it. But even for Sheryl there might come a day when playing the little woman wouldn't work, when she had to face up to the fact of being not just a woman, but a person, with some responsibility for her own destiny.

It wasn't easy, in the face of what men saw as their inalienable right to know best, as Claire was finding out. The struggle for self-determination had started long before the suffragettes chained themselves to railings in London and still continued in every woman's heart and soul.

Times had changed since the women convicts had found that without male help and sponsorship they couldn't lift themselves from a life of degradation, but remnants of the fetters of convention, of male and female role expectations, remained. And modern women sometimes tripped over them even now.

'What are you thinking about?' Gareth asked her softly, intrigued by the intensity of her expression.

'Men,' she said, giving him a clear green look, not entirely friendly. 'They've been the masters for so long they don't even recognise the whip in their hand as a whip.'

He raised his brows. 'What brought that on?'

'A train of thought,' she said. 'Too complicated to explain.'

'And do women,' he asked, 'always recognise their chains?'

She shook her head, bound to acknowledge the point. Some women, she conceded, positively revelled in theirs, or what vestiges remained to them. With sudden clarity she saw that for much of her life she, too, had defined herself in relation to men—her father, her brothers, her lovers, her husband, had shaped her behaviour, her self-image. Even her mother had seemed less a person in her own right than a shadow of her own husband. And yet her mother had defied her father in a way to keep in touch with Jess after her father had washed his hands of her.

She had always been susceptible to a surface kindness in men, to superficial charm and especially, perhaps, to admiration. Because deep down she had never thought herself an admirable, worthwhile person, deserving of the respect of others. She still didn't think it. And yet, gropingly, she was aware that being a fully functioning human being demanded self-respect above all.

The conviction had been growing for some time. It was why she had been wary of Gareth's attraction for her, why she distrusted the passion that had flowed so quickly and strongly between them. She had been only just beginning to define herself in her own terms when she met him and was plunged into an abyss of physical and emotional sensation. She had been afraid of losing herself in it, quite literally, of having her tenuous grasp on her hard-won independence ripped away, the One merged in the dual identity of the Couple.

It had happened before, with Denny, and she knew the pain of the separation when it came, like an amputation. She knew the feeling of being half of a couple, crippled, bleeding, unable to function on her own. And yet at the same time unable to function adequately in a relationship with another person. She had never been able to give herself wholly because she had not been whole.

The outer door closed as the doctor left, and shortly afterwards Pietro came back. Scott and Claire appeared behind him in the doorway, smiling, a little strained but determined to continue the party.

'It was nothing,' Claire insisted. 'I said I'd be better in a little while and I was right, see?'

'She's going to have a checkup tomorrow,' Scott added. 'But the doctor says there's no immediate worry. All the same, no more dancing for you, honey.'

He smiled down at her, and Claire smiled back, an automatic smile without radiance, but it was a smile. A beginning, Jess thought. They had hurt each other over the last two days, but they were trying to heal the wounds. She hoped that they would work it out.

Chapter Ten

Jess noticed bruises on her shoulders next morning and remembered Scott's bone-breaking grip of relief. 'Men,' she muttered to herself, ruefully touching the darkening blotches. 'They don't know their own strength, the brutes.'

She worried about Claire, wondering how she was, but for Sunday morning it was too early to phone. Anyway, if Claire was up she had probably gone to church.

Towelling her hair, she made a sudden decision to go to church herself. She hadn't been for ages, but she had regularly attended Sunday School as a child and had never entirely lost her belief, although she found it difficult to picture the Supreme Being in the terms that had been taught to her then. Still, she prayed some-times, after a fashion, and surely if there was a God He wouldn't turn a deaf ear to prayers for as dutiful a daughter as Claire, even though they came from one who was less exemplary.

The church was quite small and modern, and the service had a simplicity that Jess liked. Her prayers were clumsy, and she felt no sense of their being heard, but she emerged afterwards feeling lighter in spirit and walked home humming to herself.

She spent the rest of the morning making more notes for her book, seeing with satisfaction how the story was falling into place. With her ruminations of the night before on women's lot still fresh in mind, she began to toy with the idea of a generational saga, starting with Beth and continuing through her female descendants, tracing the story of women's gradual emancipation, not only from the physical rigours of the convict era, but also from the social and political constraints that had bound them for so long. And, ultimately, from the last emotional barriers that every woman found in her own psyche.

Grabbing a fresh piece of paper and a pencil, she began scribbling furiously, desperate to get these new insights into some kind of written form while they were still clear in her mind. She wasn't yet proficient enough on the typewriter to get the random thoughts down quickly before they dissipated.

She hardly registered the doorbell's ring, only letting out a small, exasperated sound under her breath, deciding to ignore it. When she heard Gareth's key in the lock, then vaguely realised he was standing in the doorway of the room, she said absently, 'I'm busy. Sit down,' and went back to her work.

She had covered several pages before she put down

the pencil, flexed aching fingers and looked at him, scarcely focusing on his still form on the sofa.

'I'm sorry,' he said. 'I didn't think you'd be working on a Sunday. But I suppose when the muse strikes . . .'

'Vivienne says never wait for a muse or a mood, it's a sign of amateurism. But I did feel rather inspired this morning,' she admitted, stretching her arms and easing her cramped fingers.

'And here I was thinking you were sleeping in.'

She looked at him enquiringly, and he said, 'Didn't you hear the phone? I rang at about ten.'

'Oh, I was at church.'

His brows rose. 'Is that what brought on the burst of creativity?'

'No. I don't think so. Maybe.'

He laughed, and she smiled back at him, shrugging. 'Well, I didn't go to pray for inspiration.'

'Why did you go, then?'

She shrugged again. Scott hadn't absolved her of her promise not to divulge his and Claire's problems. 'I felt like it,' she said vaguely. 'I'm not a complete heathen, you know.'

'Do you go to church often?'

'Now and then. Do you?'

'Like you, now and then. Shall we have a church wedding, Jess?'

I'd like that, she thought with surprising clarity. She and Denny had been married in a brief and bald registry office ceremony. She hadn't really felt married at all when it was over, although she had bought a special dress for the occasion and Denny had worn a flower in his buttonhole.

'What church would have us?' she asked him lightly,

embarrassed by the strength of her immediate impulse to agree eagerly. 'These days, ministers are wary of couples who want to get married in church and never darken their doors again.'

'I could ask around. And obviously we're not total unbelievers, either of us.'

'Just backsliders.'

He laughed. 'Perhaps.'

Jess turned to stack some papers together, and he said, 'If you're working, do you want me to go?'

She shook her head with some reluctance. Actually her fingers were itching to get at the typewriter. 'I just had an idea that I wanted to write down while it was fresh.'

'You certainly were immersed when I came in. I've never seen you so absorbed in anything.'

'Sorry if I was rude,' she said. 'Teach you to interrupt an artist at work.'

'Yes,' he said. 'My fault entirely. I did try to phone first, remember.'

'I'll take your word for that.'

'Thank you. Am I allowed to ask what the Great Inspiration is all about, or is it a secret?'

She hesitated. She was still shy about exposing her work to anyone, or even talking about it. But the excitement of the new direction she was taking gave her an urge to share it with someone. She told him, her eyes lit with the passion of creation, her hands emphasising her words.

When she had finished he said, 'An ambitious project for a beginner, isn't it?'

'You think I can't do it?'

'Do you think you can?'

'I don't know,' she confessed. 'All I know is I want to try.'

She was disappointed that he hadn't been more encouraging, and perhaps it showed in her face. He said, 'That's all that matters, then. I could say, "Of course you can do it," but I'm no literary expert, and I've never even seen your writing. And what difference would it make in the end? You have to believe in *yourself*, when it comes down to it, no matter what other people think.'

'Yes,' she said thoughtfully, 'you're right. But I need a publisher who believes in me, too. I don't know how Vivienne will like this new idea. It's pushing the story a lot further, in time and in . . . in dimension, than I'd thought of so far.'

'Try her. But if she says no, I'd think about getting another publisher. It sounds too good to me not to use it.'

'Do you think so?'

'I do.'

'Thank you.' On impulse she got up and walked over to him and kissed him lightly. But when she made to move away he grabbed her wrist and pulled her down onto his knee, grinning. 'You needn't think you're getting away with that. Kiss me properly.'

'I don't give in to orders,' she retorted, squirming on his lap and turning her head to avoid his mouth. 'Besides, it's past lunchtime and I'm hungry.'

'Mm, so am I.' His teeth grazed her throat, nipping lightly, and she gurgled, 'Good heavens, you should have told me you were a vampire!'

'You taste delicious,' he said, shifting his hands to her throat and holding her arched over the arm of the sofa, her head tipping back while his tongue darted into the little hollow at the base of her throat, feeling the accelerated pulse beat there. It was highly erotic but not a comfortable position to remain in, and although she suffered it for a while, soon she began trying to wriggle free.

His hands went to her shoulders, gripping firmly to keep her still, and she yelped with pain.

He let go immediately, the laughter in his face replaced with concern. 'I'm *sorry,* Jess! What did I do? I didn't mean to hurt you.'

'It's all right,' she said, standing up. 'I've got a bruise, that's all—banged into a door this morning. If you've finished asserting your macho image, I'll get us some lunch.'

Following her into the kitchen, he asked, 'Are you sure you're all right?'

'Yes, stop feeling guilty. You weren't to know. The bread's a bit stale. How would cream cheese and ham on toast suit you?'

'Fine,' he said. 'I promise I'll treat you like glass from now on.'

She slanted a mocking glance at him. 'I may hold you to that.'

She had a countertop gadget that browned open sandwiches nicely, and she made the toast, spread cheese thickly on top and laid slices of ham over it before returning them to the grill. As she stood watching them, Gareth slid his arms about her waist from behind, kissing her neck softly, and she leaned back against him, enjoying the sensation. When she realised that he was opening her zipper she made a move of protest, but he didn't stop, saying in her ear, his voice teasing, 'I'll kiss it better for you, Jess.'

She was half turning to stop him as he eased the material away from her shoulder, revealing her bra strap and the telltale bluish fingermarks that marred her skin. She saw the sudden shock in his face, and then he jerked the other side of her dress down, inspecting the marks with narrowed eyes, knowing what they were, knowing she had lied.

When his eyes met hers they were full of accusation, and she said faintly, her own eyes widening in apprehension, 'Glass, remember, Gareth?'

The smell of burning suddenly registered from behind her and blue smoke wreathed about them. She exclaimed, 'The toast!' and he muffled a curse and let her swing about. She tried to hunch the dress back into place while hastily removing the scorched slices from the grill, shaking her fingers after she had dropped the toast on the counter.

'It's not so bad,' she said breathlessly, afraid to look at him, trying to fill the ominous silence with words. 'Just the edges are a bit black, that's all. I'll cut them off and it'll still be quite edible.' She picked up a knife and began industriously sawing off the charred crusts. 'Do me up, please, Gareth,' she asked him, her voice casual, her hand on the knife showing white knuckles.

For a second there was no response. Then the zipper was closed with a decisive movement. She heard him move away, and nearly sighed audibly with relief. She placed the toasted slices on the plates, fixed a smile on her face and turned to put the food on the table. Gareth was standing at the other side of it with a glacial expression. As she put her hand on the chair back to pull it out and sit down, he said, 'Just what kind of door did you bang into, Jess?'

Her fingers gripped the chair. 'It was Scott,' she said,

not looking at him. 'But it wasn't the way it looks, Gareth.'

'Then why lie to me about it?'

He had a point there. It hadn't been a premeditated lie. 'I don't know,' she answered truthfully, looking up at him at last. 'Probably because I was afraid you'd react just the way you are now.'

'I've never thought of myself as a particularly jealous man,' he said thoughtfully.

Jess's smile was wry. 'No?'

His own mouth relaxed a fraction into not quite a smile. 'I might not have reacted so strongly if you hadn't been dishonest about it in the first place. Do you want to tell me what really happened?'

'He was under stress,' she said. 'He needed something to hold on to. I happened to be nearest, that's all.'

'I have a feeling it's a whole lot more complicated than that,' Gareth said wryly. 'But I guess it at least approximates the truth. I shouldn't ask this, but I have to . . . Did he kiss you?'

Jess shook her head, her eyes fearlessly meeting his. 'I told you, it was nothing like that.'

He nodded, apparently satisfied, and she pulled out the chair and sat down. With her eyes on her plate she said, 'I'm sorry, Gareth. It was stupid of me to lie. I won't do it again.'

He sat down, too, and put a hand across the table to hold hers. Obeying a sudden desire to make amends, she lifted their linked fingers to her bent head and kissed his hand. His fingers tightened, and she looked up, surprising a strange expression in his eyes. Colour stained his cheekbones and he said huskily, 'You shouldn't do that.'

Daring to tease, she put her head to one side and

said pertly, 'Why not? I think it has an interesting effect on you.'

'It has an effect on me that you don't begin to understand,' he answered, and took his hand away to pick up a knife and cut into the toast.

After lunch he suggested going out somewhere. They went out often, to be alone but in public, and though neither said anything, they both knew why. Jess was relieved that Gareth had accepted her terms for their engagement, and somewhat surprised that he was scrupulous in helping her to avoid too many private occasions when they might be tempted to give in to the sexual tension that was ever-present between them.

This time Jess refused, and finally told him bluntly that she wanted to get on with her writing while the urge stayed with her.

'You're not making excuses, are you?' he asked sceptically.

'I just want to work!' she said. 'I know you don't take my writing seriously, but . . .'

'Hey, hey!' he objected. 'Who says I don't? I know it's important to you. If you want to be left alone, you only have to say so.'

'I just did!' she said, glaring at him. 'And you accused me of making excuses.'

'Asked, not accused. I'm going. Let's not start a fight, Jess. What about next Sunday then? Can I count on spending the day with you?'

'I suppose so,' she said ungraciously. He laughed at her, kissed her cheek and said, 'I'll keep you to that, then, muse or no muse.' And left her.

She phoned Scott first, learning that Claire seemed all right but tired, and was resting. Then she worked for hours, and later telephoned Vivienne at home and arranged to meet the editor the following morning at her city office.

Vivienne seemed rather doubtful of the plans Jess outlined for the expansion of her novel, and Jess was a little dashed, her enthusiastic confidence beginning to waver.

'Don't you think I could do it?' she asked.

Vivienne looked consideringly at her. 'I don't know,' she said frankly. 'If you bring it off it could be a much better book than the one you were going to write. The question is, can you handle the material?'

'I think so,' Jess said. 'I know I'm a novice, but I feel this is how I really want to tackle it now. It's taking shape in my mind so powerfully.'

'Put it on paper for me,' Vivienne said, 'and I'll think about it.'

Afterwards Jess bought a snack lunch and ate it at Dawes Point Park in the shadow of the bridge, before walking to the State Archives building at The Rocks, its architecture carefully designed to blend with the irregular roofs and asymetrical facades of the older buildings surrounding it.

Summer proper was nearly over, but the heat of the day shimmered off the pavements and created dazzling lights on the water of the harbour, and she was tempted to give up the idea of poring over dusty documents. Sydney's climate and the numerous beaches that indented its harbour and the coastline north and south of the city induced a hedonistic spirit in its inhabitants. Not only on weekends, but every day for seven balmy months of the year, the sand and the surf beckoned, and there were always those who seemed to have nothing better to do than to laze about soaking up the sun and riding the Pacific rollers.

Jess had often been among them, but now she had a serious purpose in life, she reminded herself. Well, a purpose, anyway, she amended with a small grin at her own pretension. Taking up the bag containing her notebooks and pens, she steadfastly turned her back on the enticements of the sea.

By the end of the day her strong-mindedness was vindicated by the discovery of an old diary that gave her a new picture of life on a bush farm in the 1800s. As excited as an adventurer finding long-buried treasure, she lost all sense of time and place. Here was a vivid record of a pioneer family clearing and felling the bush, cutting trees that sported strange, narrow foliage tending to grey-blues rather than greens and never lost their leaves; trying to grow crops in a huge, empty new country where the relentless summer sun dried out all ground vegetation to a uniform yellowish brown and the rain, when it came, arrived not in showers but in torrents.

The next day she roughed out some more chapters, and that evening she worked late preparing another written outline for Vivienne, to post the next morning. She was tidying the pages to put them into an envelope when the doorbell rang.

'Scott!' she said, as she opened the door for him. 'Is something wrong? Come in.'

'I have to talk to someone, Jess,' he said. 'Do you mind? I know it's late.'

He looked dreadful, his skin sallow and his eyes glazed, without their usual vivid clarity.

'What's happened?' she asked, taking his arm to lead him into the living room. 'Claire?'

'It's okay,' he said quickly. 'There's no immediate crisis. She's in hospital for observation and tests. I hung about as long as they'd let me, then went for a walk. I've walked miles, and when I found myself near here, I thought you might still be up.'

'It wouldn't have mattered if I wasn't,' she said softly. 'Sit down, Scott, I'll get you a cup of coffee. Unless you want something stronger?'

He shook his head, sinking wearily down on the sofa. 'Coffee will be fine, thanks.'

She made some toasted sandwiches and took them in with the coffee, guessing that he probably hadn't eaten.

'You're an angel, Jess,' he said after a second cup of coffee, refusing the last sandwich on the plate.

He looked much better, his colour returning to normal and his eyes showing more life, though his expression was still grim.

'You can't be yourself,' she teased. 'You know I'm nothing of the sort.'

He grinned at her with something like his normal humour. 'In disguise,' he said. 'No, really, Jess, I'm grateful. For what you did the other night, too.'

'I didn't do anything except point out to Claire that she could see a specialist without committing herself to anything. Has she seen someone today? Is that why she's in hospital?'

'Yes, she has. Pietro's doctor was pretty worried, I think, though he wanted me to keep it from her. He got onto her doctor and she saw a cardiologist this afternoon.'

'A heart specialist?'

Scott nodded. 'First of all they want to find out what sort of condition her heart is in. Then they'll start investigating other things. I only hope she'll be sensible if . . .'

'Don't count on it, Scott,' she warned. 'Claire wants her child to live and,' she said slowly, 'surely she has a right to make her own decision.'

'At the cost of her *life?*'

'If she's willing to take that risk.'

He said accusingly, 'I thought you were fond of Claire.'

'I am. And she has the right to have that baby if she wants it, Scott!' Jess said unequivocally.

For a moment he was silent. Then he said bitingly, 'That's crazy. I can only suppose the fact that you can't have babies of your own is warping your judgment.'

Jess's eyes dilated before she dropped her lashes over them, looking down at her hands.

Scott said, 'Oh, God, I'm sorry, Jess. I guess I don't know what I'm saying. I didn't mean it.'

'That's all right,' she said huskily. 'I know how you feel. I know how Claire feels, too. I love you both.'

'Forgive me?'

'I told you, it's all right.' She got up to take the empty coffee cup away, and he stood up, too, clumsily. But he didn't follow her into the kitchen, and when she returned he was still standing where she had left him, looking oddly lost, as though he didn't know whether to go or to stay.

With an urge to comfort, she went to him and put her arms around him, and he made an inarticulate sound and hugged her tightly, his cheek against hers moist with tears. Wrung with pity, she held him mutely until he broke away, dashing the back of his hand over his eyes and smiling wryly at her as he lightly touched her cheek with the other hand.

'Would you like to stay the night?' she asked impulsively. Catching the surprise in his eyes, she added hastily, 'I've got a camp bed we could set up in this room if you don't want to be at home alone.'

'Thanks,' he said, 'but I've imposed on you enough. And just in case the hospital rings I'd better be at home.'

He phoned a taxi, and as they waited for it, he said jerkily, 'I vowed to love and cherish her, Jess. That's what I want to do . . . what I *must* do. Even if it goes against what she wants. I'm responsible for her; she's my wife.'

'Who's responsible for you, Scott?' Jess asked him.

He frowned. 'I am, of course,' he said shortly. Seeing the sardonic lift of her eyebrows, he added, 'Okay, so equality doesn't come into it. I'm afraid I don't care. All I care about is that she doesn't die.'

'I think you're wrong,' she said softly. But she could see he wouldn't listen.

Claire, out of the bitterness of their first real quarrel, had been a little hard on him last night, but basically her assessment was right. Scott had always got what he wanted, one way or another. He had even got Claire, the unattainable woman who had wanted to dedicate her life to God in a convent. He loved her, and now he was riding roughshod over her wishes for her own sake. He was even willing to lose her love if it meant saving her life.

The following Sunday when Gareth asked her where she would like to go, she suggested the re-created Old

Sydney Town at Somersby. Wandering among family groups and camera-hung tourists, they studied the sailing ships anchored near the town, watched a cooper dressed in eighteenth-century breeches and stockings plying his ancient trade, and visited the working windmill, like those that had once dotted the slopes above Sydney. 'Soldiers' and 'settlers' and 'convicts' in appropriate garb went about their business, lending an air of authenticity that gave the visitors the impression of having been landed by a time capsule into another era, and during the afternoon there was an alarm given when a 'convict' ran through the streets, hunted by a red-coated 'soldiers' waving their muskets and demanding the assistance of the public. Entering into the spirit of things, some helped and some hindered the guards, until the 'felon' was apprehended and summarily dealt with in the 'magistrate's court,' after which there followed a reenactment of a flogging at the triangle, which Jess elected to miss.

Gareth said, 'Don't you think you should take notes?'

'It isn't genuine, anyway,' she said. 'And after reading about the effects of the real thing as carried out in the old days, I don't find anything particularly entertaining about the performance of a mock one.'

She did make a few notes on the artifacts preserved in the printery, the coach house and the blacksmith's shop.

'A bit difficult,' Gareth commented, 'to soak up the genuine atmosphere with all these people about.'

'Oh, I don't know,' Jess replied. 'There were a lot of people about in the original old town. I'm just trying to imagine them all in the clothes of the time.' She grinned at his expression as a teenage couple in jeans, arms entwined, passed by with a blaring transistor radio.

He looked down at her. 'I can't see you in convict dress,' he said. 'You'd have been wearing silk in the latest fashion.'

'Probably provided by some barracks officer,' she retorted. 'I can just see you in uniform: red jacket, polished buttons and epaulettes. You'd definitely look the part.'

'And would you have deigned to be my mistress, my proud beauty?' he asked, twirling an imaginary moustache.

'I probably wouldn't have had much choice,' she answered. 'If I hadn't already been raped on the ship on the way out, it was just as likely to happen at the women's factory or even on the way there. It was an overnight trip by boat then, with guards. And the soldiers weren't renowned for their refinement. I'd have had to settle for you as the lesser of several evils. If virtuous females were as few and far between as some of the early moralists thought, the women were hardly to blame. Any man who offered a clean dress, a roof and soap and water, not to mention a guaranteed food supply, must have looked like a saviour to those women, even if he didn't offer them a marriage license as well.'

'Yes, I suppose he would,' Gareth said. 'I don't know that I'd appreciate being regarded as a lesser evil, though.'

'Every man is a lesser evil,' she said crushingly. 'Sometimes I think it would be infinitely preferable to get along entirely without them.'

'Watch it,' he said. 'Your cynicism is showing. Anyway, men often feel the same way about women. Life might be simpler that way, but much less interesting, don't you think?'

On the way home they went for a short walk in the Ku-ring-gai Chase National Park. The late afternoon sun filtered silver through the high, stiff leaves of the gum trees. Narrow runnels of water coursed between shallow banks bordered by ferns and starry wild flowers. The loudest sound was the harsh chatter of a kookaburra laughing invisibly somewhere nearby as they passed, and the only other life they saw, in spite of the many cars that had been parked at the beginning of the trail, were a small wallaby hopping across their path to disappear into the bush, and a lizard basking on a sunlit rock.

When they sat down to rest, leaning against the aromatic, peeling bark of a red gum tree, Jess sighed. 'It's so lovely, I could stay here forever.'

'Mm, peaceful, isn't it?' Gareth agreed, watching a brilliantly plumaged rosella flitting across the open space between two trees. 'Of course, there could be a snake or two around.'

'Beast,' Jess said absently. 'I don't care. Anyway, if I keep perfectly still—and I've no desire at the moment to do otherwise—they won't even realise I'm alive. They can slide straight over me and go on their way.'

He took her wrist in a cool, firm hand, feeling for her pulse. 'You're alive,' he informed her.

'You're not a snake.'

'Thanks for that, anyway.'

She smiled and closed her eyes, slipping into a light doze. When she woke, only minutes later, he was watching her, her hand still held in his.

'Jess,' he said, 'I'm taking advantage, perhaps, of

that promise you made me earlier. Why can't you have children? Is it accidental or . . . deliberate?'

'Deliberate? No!' Oddly wounded, her voice rising with quick hostility, she said, 'Why do you think that?'

'I don't think it. I'm only asking.'

'It was the car crash,' she said baldly. 'I was pregnant then, and it killed the baby and . . . I was a mess. They had to do an operation. It means I can never conceive again.'

He lifted her hand to his cheek. 'I'm so sorry, darling,' he said, his eyes filled with compassion. 'It must have been rough on you.'

'I got over it,' she said hardily. But, unexpectedly, hot tears gushed into her eyes and poured down her cheeks. She raised her free hand to hide them, to try to brush them away, but they kept coming, and she sobbed, frustratedly shaking her head, thinking herself a complete and utter fool.

Chapter Eleven

$\mathcal{G}$areth pulled her into his arms and stroked her hair, saying he was sorry, that he hadn't wanted to upset her.

She realised that his caressing hands were unsteady, and clutched at him, trying to tell him it wasn't his fault. When the storm of weeping had passed, she pressed one of his hands to her hot cheek and said, 'I don't know why I did that. It's so long ago. You must think I'm an idiot.'

'Darling,' he groaned, 'you don't have to *apologise* to me.' Stroking her hair, he kissed her temple and said, 'Did you cry when it happened?'

'Oh, yes,' she said. 'Lots.' But never as freely, she realised. She had wept quietly in corners, trying to hide her continuing grief from Denny because it irritated him, made him feel embarrassed and guilty.

'I must look awful.' She sniffed inelegantly. 'You're

supposed to have offered me a clean white handkerchief from your breast pocket by now.'

'Sorry, my handkerchief's in the pocket of my jacket, and I left that in the car.'

Sighing elaborately, Jess got to her feet. 'I always pick the wrong men,' she complained. 'You'd think I'd have learned by now.'

'Shall I tear my shirt into strips for you?' he offered. 'Though you've already soaked it fairly thoroughly.' He looked down ruefully at the wet stain on the blue cotton.

'Noble of you,' Jess said, grateful to him for following her lead, 'but that's bandages you're thinking of. Perhaps I could tear up my petticoat, if I had one.' She delicately wiped her nose on the back of her hand.

'You tantalise the imagination. What else are you not wearing, I wonder?'

Jess choked on a slightly watery laugh. 'Don't get excited. Maybe I should get a chastity belt.'

'The husband keeps the key,' he reminded her. 'And I'm going to be your husband, remember?'

She hadn't forgotten, and right now the word had a comforting ring of security and warmth. He put his arm about her waist and they walked back to the car together. 'I really need a cigarette,' she told him as she slid into her seat.

'We don't have any,' he said. 'Besides, you've given them up.'

'I *know*.' She raised her eyes and clenched her fists and her teeth dramatically. 'But I *need* a cigarette!'

'You don't need it, you only want it. Willpower,' he advised callously.

'What would you know about it?'

'Quite a lot, as a matter of fact.' His eyes held hers. 'I've had to exercise mine fairly often lately.'

'Ohhh, have the last word then,' she conceded. She fished her makeup and a tissue out of her bag, wiped her nose properly and repaired some of the ravages from her bout of tears.

When he said, 'Ready?' she smiled and nodded. For a moment longer he regarded her, concern and tenderness in his eyes. Then he leaned over and kissed her, touching her only with his lips, light, lingering, persuasive and compassionate, all at once. Her mouth parted on a silent sigh of contentment and pleasure, and when they drew apart she lay with her head still turned to him and said, 'Gareth?'

'Yes?' He was smiling at her, his eyes lazy.

'Will you . . .' She paused, moistening her lips with the tip of her tongue. Her mouth was dry. 'Will you,' she repeated, 'teach me to drive?'

He said, 'Yes, of course. Want to start now?' as though it was a perfectly natural request and there had never been any discussion between them about it. That made it easier for her to say, 'Why not?' And if he thought her tone overcareless he didn't show it, merely getting out of the driver's seat and allowing her to slide across to it while he went round the car to sit beside her.

She was nervous, but not as terrified as she had feared. And he was a very good teacher, patient, clear and watchful.

He let her go through the gears as many times as she wanted before they started moving, and didn't try to make her carry on when she said she had had enough.

'After such a historic day,' he said, 'I feel we ought to

celebrate in an appropriate fashion. How about dinner at the Waterfront?'

Jess accepted the idea with enthusiasm but said, 'Take me home first, though; I want to wash and change.'

'You look fine to me,' he said, but did as she asked.

She wore a black dress with a low neck and no back, and when he saw it he said, 'I hope you've got your chastity belt on; you may need it.'

She laughed at him and threw a pale silky cream shawl about her shoulders, laughing again as he gave an exaggerated whistle of relief.

The Waterfront Restaurant was a converted warehouse in the once notorious area of The Rocks, now being restored. They dined on the outdoor plaza with a view of the glittering fantastical wings of the Opera House and the light-strung arch of the Harbour Bridge. Squeamishly, Jess declined to choose a lobster from the giant tank near the entrance, and Gareth also opted for another item on the menu.

'Are you sufficiently steeped in history?' he asked her after they had had drinks in the Wharf Bar, where the decorations included ship's lanterns and boats, and the bar itself was made of wooden logs with a canopy of old sails.

'I think I've had sufficient of everything,' she said. 'That was a wonderful meal, and it's been a lovely day. Thank you, Gareth.'

'My pleasure. Want to go?'

'I'll give you coffee,' she promised.

'I don't think so. Tonight I will bid you a chaste farewell on your doorstep; otherwise I won't be responsible for my actions. I told you what that dress does to me.'

Apparently he meant it, too, for he kissed her very briefly and left before she had time to give way to the temptation to entice him in anyway and see what happened. Just as well, too, she told herself. Tomorrow she wanted to be up carly to go back to The Rocks and spend some time in the State Archives, researching another aspect of her book.

Her contract arrived and she called Gareth and asked him to look it over because Vivienne had advised her to get her lawyer to vet it before signing.

'Will tomorrow evening be okay?' he asked.

'Yes, fine. Shall I bring it round to your place?'

'You can do that when you have your license and a car,' he told her. 'I'll come and pick you up, look at the contract and give you another driving lesson, okay?'

'Okay,' she agreed, smiling. 'I'll look forward to that.'

'Well, good.' He sounded agreeably surprised, perhaps understandably, since she had shown such reluctance to learn to drive. In fact she was still horribly scared but determined not to show it.

The lesson, in the event, came first, and she became less unsure all the time, eventually drawing up outside her house and putting on the brake with a sense of triumph.

Gareth glanced over the contract afterwards, suggested she query Vivienne on one or two points and said, 'Otherwise, it seems pretty fair and straightforward to me. Have you asked her about the changes you want to make in the book?'

'Yes. She hasn't committed herself, she's a bit doubtful about it. I think I'll leave signing until she decides.'

'Good thinking. Any chance of a coffee?'

'Of course.' She got up to make it, and he strolled into the kitchen, leaning on the counter and watching her with undisguised pleasure.

'You'll make me nervous, staring like that,' she told him.

'You ought to be used to being stared at. You know, I think you get more beautiful every time I look at you.'

Maybe I do, she thought. Certainly his attention made her more aware of herself, brought her singingly alive all through. 'The eye of the beholder,' she said, placing the steaming cups on the table. 'Come and get it.'

'You ought to be more careful with your invitations,' he said, coming round behind her and dropping a quick kiss on the curve of her neck before sliding into his chair.

'*You* ought to be more careful with your conclusions,' she told him. 'Lawyers are supposed to be cautious types.'

'You bring out the reckless streak in me.'

'Yes, I do, don't I?' She eyed him thoughtfully. 'You never really intended to propose to me, did you?'

'That's a leading question. If you mean when we first met, I suppose not. Most people don't make their minds up that quickly.'

'I mean when we first made love.'

He frowned a little, then grinned. 'To tell you the truth, I had more immediate things in mind then. Does it matter?'

Jess shrugged. 'I guess not.'

'Come on,' he said. 'What's bothering you, Jess?'

'Nothing. Drink your coffee before it gets cold.'

He gave her an exasperated look before lifting his cup to his lips.

The telephone broke into the silence, and almost gratefully she rose to answer it.

'Scott!' she said as his voice greeted her, and she saw Gareth turn in his chair, listening. 'How's Claire?'

'They say she should have an operation,' he said baldly, his voice strained.

Jess gasped. 'What kind of operation?'

Gareth's cup thudded down on the table, and he got up and came over to her, his eyes incredulous.

Scott was saying, 'She's seen an obstetrician and a cardiac surgeon. The operation is to replace the damaged valve with an artificial one. It's open heart surgery, but according to the doctors it's less dangerous for both Claire and the baby to have this done and continue the pregnancy than it is to put her through the trauma of either an abortion or labour without it. With the new valve, they say the heart should function normally.'

'Well . . . of course there's always a risk with surgery of any kind, isn't there? But, Scott, aren't you glad?'

He hesitated. 'I think Claire has convinced the obstetrician that she would do anything to save the child.'

'You've always known that,' Jess reminded him.

'Yes,' he agreed. 'You're right. Well, I thought you'd want to know. It's to be sometime next month. Until then she can come home as long as she rests and takes the medication they're giving her.'

'Can I visit her?'

'Of course. She'd like that.'

'Give her my love, Scott.'

Gareth said as she put down the receiver, '*An operation?* And Scott's supposed to be *glad?*'

Jess shook her head. 'You only heard half the

conversation. Well, you might as well know now, I suppose. Claire needs an operation on her heart. Her doctor thought an abortion might be indicated, and of course she wouldn't consent to that. Now it seems that it isn't necessary, anyway. They say they can repair the damaged heart and still save the baby.'

'I knew nothing about this.'

'Maybe I shouldn't have told you, but since you heard what you did . . .'

'I won't pass it on.'

'I know you won't. And I knew you'd be concerned about Claire.'

'Naturally. Is that why she was feeling rocky at the party?'

'Probably. Scott was frantic.'

'Yes, so would I have been in his place.'

I'm sure you would, Jess thought. She flickered a curious look at him and saw that his face was grim, his eyes sombre. 'The doctors say she'll be all right,' she assured him softly.

'I suppose Scott will have got the very best medical advice, anyway,' Gareth said frowningly.

'Yes of course,' she answered. 'I'm sure she'll be all right, Gareth.' She tried to sound as confident as she could.

Claire seemed genuinely confident. 'The specialists explained it to me very carefully,' she said when Jess went to see her. 'It used to be thought that pregnancy was too great a strain for anyone with a heart condition like mine, but it's been shown that's not so.'

'Oh.' Jess tried not to show scepticism in her face.

'There's a ninety-five percent chance of the operation

succeeding, especially in my case, because it's a simple aortic valve replacement, not a multiple one like some people have, and I'm young and otherwise fit. Afterwards I'll be on some medication for a while—although they have to take care what they use because of the baby—and I should be able to have a perfectly normal labour and delivery when the time comes.'

'So, you don't need to risk your life for your baby, after all?'

'No. Anyway, Dr. Phillips says nowadays there's no question of having to choose between saving the mother or the child. The thing is for the heart specialist to treat the disease and the obstetrician to look after the baby.'

'Then Scott must be feeling a lot better about things?'

'Yes. I asked Dr. Phillips to talk to him, and he seemed . . . satisfied. Enough about my troubles, anyway, Jess. How's the book coming along?'

Jess looked at her thoughtfully, thinking that something still wasn't right here, but that it wasn't her business, so she accepted the change of subject. Vivienne had cautiously accepted the latest outline, and the contract had been duly signed and delivered. An advance, she had been told, would be on its way.

The cheque from the publishers arrived quite soon, and she was so excited that when Gareth came in the same evening she called to him from the bedroom where she was changing, 'Have a look on my desk. My first advance is there!'

Seconds later she emerged to see him holding two cheques in his hand, and without thought she crossed the room to whip the other one out of his hand, saying, 'No, not that one.' It was Denny's maintenance cheque.

'Sorry,' he said. His face was wooden. 'You'd better bank this.' Then, as though against his better judgement, he said, 'And you can give up the other now, can't you? You won't be needing his money anymore.'

'On the strength of one small advance?' She raised her brows.

'On the strength of that and the fact that we'll be married in a couple of months' time. After which, if you don't earn enough to keep yourself, *I* will be maintaining you.'

'In the style to which I'm accustomed?'

'Possibly not,' he said evenly, 'judging by the size of that cheque. Will it matter?'

She said, 'No.' And, looking at the hard scepticism in his face, she tore the cheque in two, then in two again. 'There,' she said, handing him the pieces. 'Throw them in the wastebasket for me, will you?'

He took the torn scraps, looking slightly dazed. 'You didn't have to do that.'

'Yes I did,' she said. 'We'd have been having a fight in a minute.'

He started to say, 'No . . .' Then he crushed the pieces of paper in his hand and a faint colour came into his cheeks. 'Yes, we probably would. I'm sorry, Jess. I shouldn't have said anything about it.'

'No, you shouldn't,' she agreed. 'I told you once before, I don't feel any guilt about taking Denny's money. He let me down when I needed him. He . . . damn him, he was *responsible* for the accident that lost us our baby. I've never said that before. I kept pretending he wasn't at fault because I knew he couldn't take it. Guilt isn't something Denny's equipped to cope with. He wouldn't even accept any of the blame for the breakup of our marriage.'

Gareth was looking at her with faint surprise. She made a helpless, impatient gesture with one hand. 'Oh, I'm not saying I mightn't have done more. Maybe I should have tried harder, made a greater effort to get over the accident, the baby, the fact that I could never have a child again. . . . I could have been more forgiving. I suppose in a way I've been punishing him all these years, taking his money . . . I haven't even used a lot of it. Not that he's missed it much. But I felt he owed me that. At least he owed me *something* in . . . compensation for what he'd taken from me.'

Gareth listened in silence, his eyes unreadable, almost grey, the blue colour washed out of them. Jess flicked a glance at him, then laughed a little. 'I'm not a nice person,' she said. 'Am I? Want to change your mind about marrying me?'

She was half serious, half afraid that maybe now that he knew how mean and vengeful her inner motives could be he might not want her as his wife.

He tossed the pieces of the cheque into the basket as she had instructed, and came towards her, taking her face in his hands. 'You asked me that before, and the answer's still the same. I won't change my mind,' he said. 'What about you?'

She looked up at him and felt a strange sensation of melting inside. 'Not on your life,' she said fervently. 'You're the catch of the year, and I'm a twenty-eight-year-old, slightly used single woman. I'm not about to pass up the best offer I've had yet.'

He laughed and kissed her. 'Am I the best offer?'

'Definitely,' she said firmly. 'There weren't too many in the honourable class.' Plenty of the other kind, but she didn't need to tell him that.

'This book you're writing,' Mrs. Seymour said the next time Gareth took Jess to Karunja. 'It's a history, is it?'

'Not exactly.' Jess took one of the dainty butterfly cream cakes she was offered, and then wished she hadn't. With her tea, in one of Mrs. Seymour's exquisite bone china cups, in one hand, and the cake in the other, she said, 'It's going to be a novel now.'

'Oh,' Gareth's mother said. 'Fiction.'

'Yes.'

'Well, I'm sure,' Mrs. Seymour said, 'it won't be one of those so-called historical sagas that are full of sex and nastiness.' She didn't sound sure; she sounded somewhat desperately hopeful.

Carefully Jess said, 'Well, there was rather a lot of it about at the time.'

Gareth, sitting next to Jess on the brocade chaise, hid a smile, and his father laughed.

'I daresay there was,' Mrs. Seymour conceded. 'But I have never seen the necessity for authors to wallow in such things. Personally I prefer a nice clean book with decent morals.'

Rather dryly, Jess said, 'I don't intend to wallow in anything, but a writer can hardly ignore the seamier side of life or gloss over it. I want to tell people how it really was.'

Mr. Seymour nodded. 'If all the nasty bits were suppressed there wouldn't be any story, would there? You can't tell much about the struggle between good and evil if you don't mention the evil.'

'Well, of course,' his wife said pacifically, deferring to the male view. 'Provided one doesn't overstep the bounds of good taste.'

Whose bounds? Jess thought, fairly certain that Mrs. Seymour's ideas of good taste were miles apart from her own. Don't start an argument, her better self warned.

She bit viciously into the cream cake, filling her mouth with it so that she wouldn't be tempted to return to the debate. She found these afternoon teas excruciating, but Mrs. Seymour apparently felt obliged to invite her, and the least she could do was try to fulfil the minimum social obligations of a future daughter-in-law. This sort of thing had not arisen with Denny; his parents were divorced, and both had remarried and had fairly hectic social lives of their own.

She washed the cake down with tea, wishing for a glass of whisky, which she had never been offered in this house—Mrs. Seymour evidently being persuaded that ladies didn't indulge—and tried to concentrate on the gist of the conversation.

'Your parents,' Mrs. Seymour said to Jess. 'Do they never come to Sydney?'

Jess shook her head. 'Not for years.'

'But surely for your wedding?'

'Oh, that wasn't . . .' Jess stopped, flushing. 'Oh, you mean my wedding to Gareth.'

'That was what I meant, yes,' his mother said frostily. 'Gareth tells me you plan to be married in Sydney.'

She hadn't thought of anything else—certainly not of going 'home' to be married, even if her parents would have had her.

'Yes, I suppose so,' she said vaguely, giving him a slightly agonised glance.

'We hope to find a suitable church,' he said smoothly. 'I've been making enquiries.'

'Yes, well, *our* vicar, of course, won't marry a divorced person, I'm afraid,' Mrs. Seymour said with firm regret.

'I know, I asked,' Gareth said shortly.

Jess laid one arm along the back of the chaise, crossing her legs and swinging one foot in its high-heeled sandal, her eyes half closed.

Gareth got to his feet, taking her hand to pull her up with him. 'Come on, you promised me a game of tennis. Go and get changed. You can use Fiona's room—can't she, Mother?'

Mrs. Seymour barely managed a punctilious smile. 'Yes, of course.'

On the grass court, Jess played with a good deal of vigour, her shots zinging over the net like bullets, and came close to beating Gareth. 'One day I'll win,' she promised him as they relaxed on the grass together, shaded by a rough-barked pepper tree.

'You almost did,' he admitted. 'You had me working pretty hard there. Being in a temper does wonders for your game.'

'Who's in a temper?'

'You were. Don't mind Mother too much. She really didn't mean to be tactless.'

Jess didn't answer that, and after a few minutes he said, 'Wouldn't you like to have your parents here for the wedding?'

'No.'

'I'd like to meet them.'

She looked at him. 'No, you wouldn't.'

'But I would,' he insisted. 'Why don't we fly up there

one weekend and invite them in person to come to our wedding?'

'Because,' she said, sitting up and glaring at him, 'there's no point and I don't want to. You wouldn't like them, anyway. They're very boring people.'

She had shocked him, she saw. He would never have spoken disparagingly of his own parents, and she felt a twinge of shame. Jumping to her feet, she said defiantly, 'I'm thirsty. Can I have a proper drink, do you suppose?'

'Yes, of course,' he said politely, and she wanted to despise him for not speaking his mind, for adopting the mask of the courteous host that showed up her own lack of manners. Instead she was miserably aware of his displeasure, and totally unable to display the necessary contrition to allay it.

Chapter Twelve

The phone call came like a judgement. The bell was ringing insistently when Gareth brought her home that evening, and when she picked up the receiver, she at first didn't even recognise her brother's voice. But the words were all too clear. 'Dad's had a stroke,' Ralph told her tersely. 'Mum thinks you should be here.'

'How is she?' she asked automatically. Then, 'How serious is it? Is he dying?'

'We don't know yet,' Ralph said. 'He's unconscious. Mum's bearing up. We're both with her. But she wants you to come.'

She wants you to come.

'She wants me to come,' she repeated to Gareth as soon as she had told him the bald facts. 'Why?'

He frowned, looking for once at a loss, obviously not understanding her. 'You're their daughter. Naturally they want you.'

'Yes,' she said vaguely. 'I suppose I ought . . .'

'I'll book a flight,' he said and reached for the phone. She heard him asking for two seats on the earliest possible plane the next morning, and when he put down the receiver she said, 'Two?'

'I'm coming with you,' he told her firmly. 'But it means I'll have to go in to the office tonight. Will you be all right?'

'Yes.' She was surprised. 'Why shouldn't I be?'

'You've had a shock. Shall I make you a cup of tea or something?'

She shook her head. 'I'm all right. I can fly up there on my own, you know. You needn't hold my hand.'

'I'm coming,' he reiterated.

'Oh, well . . . you said you wanted to meet them, didn't you?'

'Not in these circumstances, though.'

'Still, you usually get your own way in the end.'

He cast her an exasperated, puzzled glance and said, 'You'd better get some rest. I'll pick you up early in the morning, at six, okay?'

She nodded; then he kissed her cheek and let himself out.

Their house looked smaller than she remembered. Her mother had aged, faded somehow, and she cried when Jess awkwardly kissed her cheek. Feeling tears pricking at her own eyelids, Jess despised herself for sentimentality, and turned to greet her brother Ralph and his wife, who were standing by smiling stiffly, and to introduce Gareth.

Bill was at the hospital, they said. Her father had regained consciousness but was not responding. Ralph had been about to take his mother back there. Perhaps Jess would like to come, too, he suggested doubtfully.

She started to shake her head, stammering, 'He might not want . . . I've only just arrived . . .'

'Perhaps Jess could have something to eat first and come along later by taxi,' Gareth said.

Gloria, Ralph's wife, said eagerly, 'Oh, you must be starving. I'll make something for you. Go on, Ralph; you take Mother and leave Jess and Gareth to me.'

She made them a nourishing light meal, and though Jess would have denied feeling hungry, she felt better when she had eaten. Gloria was very efficient. She and Ralph were staying in the house with their two children, keeping Mrs. Newall company. The children, a boy and a girl, were briefly introduced, stared with some curiosity at their 'Auntie Jess' and then went outside to play.

At the hospital, Ralph and Bill were both in the waiting room when they arrived. 'They're only letting one person see him at a time,' Ralph explained.

Bill's hair was receding already and he had put on weight. Jess felt a reluctant tug of sadness that these changes had taken place without her seeing them. He hugged her spontaneously, told her she looked great and shook Gareth's hand warmly. He was a nice person, she thought with a small shock of surprise, and he was her brother. Childhood memories came flooding back, and suddenly she was one of the family again. Her strange shyness disappeared and she was able to chat with Bill about his three small sons. 'At home with Brenda,' he said. 'Little monsters.' But the pride in his voice belied that opinion. 'Wouldn't inflict them on Mum just now. Ralph's lot's quieter.'

Then their mother came along the corridor with a nurse, saying, 'He's starting to take a bit of notice. He knew me. They say he's much better.' Jess experienced a rush of gladness and stepped forward unthinkingly to put her arm about her mother and lead her to a chair.

When she saw her father lying still against the hospital pillow, his hair greyer and sparser, his face sunken, her heart thumped painfully. This was not the stern patriarch who had called her a slut and told her he was ashamed to own her as his daughter, but a frail, sick old man whom she could only pity.

Still, it was with some trepidation that she approached the bed and stood where he could see her, looking down into his tired, bloodshot eyes. It was a moment before recognition came, and when it did there was no other emotion, no scorn, no forgiveness. Just recognition. Then he nodded slowly and whispered, 'Jess.'

'Hallo, Dad,' she said, her voice hushed. 'Mum . . . Mum asked me to come.'

For a minute there was no response. Then he nodded again and said threadily, 'Yes. Good . . . girl.'

She swallowed twice, staring at him, but he closed his eyes and seemed to be dozing, making small snuffling sounds in his throat. A nurse came by and picked up his wrist, checking it against her watch.

'He talked,' Jess said.

'That's good.' The woman smiled encouragingly. 'There may not be much damage after all.'

In the waiting room, she told them, 'He spoke to me. He said . . . something.'

Her mother began to weep quietly, and Ralph patted her shoulder.

Gareth touched Jess's arm. 'Are you okay?'

Her smile was brittle. 'Yes. I'd like to go now, though . . . unless Mum wants me to stay.'

'No, you go home,' her mother said. 'You've had a long journey. You'll see him again tomorrow. Gareth can have your room, Jess, and you can sleep with me. The children are in Bill's old room. . . .'

'I'll go to a hotel,' Gareth said. 'Then Jess can have her own room.'

'Oh, but . . .'

'Don't worry,' he said. 'We'll sort it out, and you'll have Jess with you.'

Bill drove them, and they both sat in the back seat, her limp hand held in Gareth's strong grasp. Halfway there she said, 'He called me a good girl,' and began to laugh, clamping her mouth quickly shut because the laugh was more than verging on hysterical. Tears suddenly flooded her eyes, hot and stinging, and she clenched her teeth and turned her head away so that Gareth couldn't see, not letting them fall. 'He called me a good girl,' she said again, trying for a note of humorous irony. 'I don't think,' her voice wavered in spite of herself, 'he ever said that before.'

Gareth had to return to Sydney after two days, but Jess stayed on for a further three weeks until it was certain her father would recover. His speech was slow and sometimes hesitant but otherwise unaffected, and though his right hand and arm had become useless, the physiotherapist was hopeful of some recovery. Once her father said to Jess, 'It was good of you to come. Your mother needed you.' And she replied. 'I'm glad I came.'

'That fellow,' he said. 'He was no good to you, was he?'

Denny, he meant, 'No,' she agreed.

'Knew it,' her father muttered. 'Too much money.'

Jess smiled with the kind of wry humour she had been unable to summon at the time. Her father had always distrusted moneyed people, professing a firm and pugnacious belief in the great Australian myth of a classless society, and deep suspicion of those 'well-off' few who broke the egalitarian pattern. Once she had put it down to jealousy, but there was a gritty integrity in his refusal to be impressed by what a man had. And he had stuck to his principles. When Denny had offered carelessly to 'sweeten the old man up' by setting Jess's father up in a business of his own, the refusal had been instant, unequivocal and not couched in the politest terms.

However, a swift look round the kitchen and living room of the house had shown that apparently he had allowed her mother to use the household goods and appliances that Jess had sent as presents. He might be pigheaded, rigidly moralistic and unable to admit a fault or defeat, but he was in his way a man to be respected. And now he was a man in need of compassion and softness. From somewhere she managed to find the softness that was required. She might, for those few weeks, have been almost the daughter he had wanted.

In turn, whether because of his illness or simply from having mellowed somewhat wih age, her father was far less critical than she remembered. He even seemed to approve of Gareth, who had visited him briefly. 'A lawyer, eh?' he grunted after asking him what he did for a living. 'Pays all right, does it?'

Gareth smiled. 'Fairly well. Jess won't starve, I can assure you.'

'Jess can look after herself,' her father grudgingly allowed. 'When's the wedding s'posed to be?'

'In about six weeks,' Gareth said. 'We hope you and Jess's mother will be able to come, Mr. Newall.'

Jess shot a look at him but said nothing. When they were alone later at her home he said, 'You didn't mind, did you?'

'Mind what?'

'My asking your dad to the wedding. I had the impression your feelings have changed since the last time we discussed it.'

'Well, what if they have?'

'Don't go all defensive on me, darling. I'm glad you feel better about . . . about your relationship with your family. You do, don't you?'

Jess sighed. 'Yes,' she admitted. 'They quite like you.' She looked at him speculatively and with some surprise.

'I quite like them, too.' He didn't remind her that she had predicted he would find them boring, but added with a smile, 'It may surprise you, but most people don't dislike me on sight.'

'I didn't!' she protested, reading the unspoken comment behind his words.

'No, you just didn't notice me at all.'

'Annoyed you, did it?' She looked at him from the corner of her eye, her mouth curving.

'Yes, intensely. Because I was certainly noticing you, from the moment you came up and spoke to Claire.'

'Really? Even though you were with *her*?'

'Yes, really.'

Intrigued, she would have liked to pursue the subject, but Bill came in and interrupted them and she hardly had another chance to be alone with Gareth before he left.

With his unobtrusive support withdrawn, Jess missed him more than she had thought possible. She found herself looking for him a dozen times a day, waiting for his hand to take hers in his warm, comforting clasp, his touch on her arm when she crossed the street, his quiet voice soothing her frayed nerves after a long day of going back and forth to the hospital and putting on an encouraging face for her mother.

It wasn't always easy, but as her father bent his stubborn spirit to recovery it became increasingly obvious that he wasn't going to be beaten, and even his wife began to believe that he had every chance of living an almost normal life. Jess, no longer needed but with a surprising tug of regret, made the decision to go back to Sydney. She had lost three weeks' work already on her book, and now she had a strong desire to return to it—and to Gareth.

On her arrival, she immediately phoned Scott to find out how Claire was.

'Fairly well, considering,' he told her. 'Come round and see her, why don't you? How about this evening? We've missed you.'

She rang Gareth next, told him she was home and was going to see Claire.

'I'll take you,' he offered. 'I'd like to see her myself, if it's allowed.'

As they drove across the city he said, 'I've found a minister who's willing to marry us, and a nice little church. I hope you'll approve. There's a catch of sorts, though. He says as your last wedding was a purely civil affair he regards this as your first marriage in the sight of God, that it's a solemn undertaking, et cetera, and he'd like to have a chat with us beforehand.'

'What's he like?'

'Young and a bit of a go-getter, I should say. I told him the last Saturday in June. By then your father may be fit to travel, and I thought you'd want to wait until Claire's baby is born.'

'Yes.' She looked at him gratefully. 'I'd hate Claire to miss the wedding, and I know she would, too.'

A few doors away from the Carvers' they had to draw to a halt as a vehicle came backing out of a drive. The middle-aged woman behind the wheel apparently had not seen their approach, and the car shot to the other side of the road and turned before she registered their presence with a startled look.

She wound the window down and looked out to apologise as she passed, going slowly, then her brows went up again as she said, 'Oh, it's Gareth, isn't it? What are you doing here? You didn't come to visit me?'

'Hello, Mrs. Truscott,' Gareth said. 'No, we're not visiting you, I'm afraid. I didn't know you lived here, as a matter of fact. We have friends at number fourteen.'

'Oh, yes, the Carvers. Lovely couple, and she's expecting soon, isn't she? And you . . . your mother tells me you're engaged at last. This must be your fiancée?' She peered into the car beyond him, her smile eager, and with a faint air of resignation he drew back a little to afford her a better view and said, 'This is Jess. Mrs. Truscott is a friend of my mother's, Jess.'

Jess leaned forward and gave the woman a bright, social smile, feeling distinctly foolish.

'How do you do, my dear!' Mrs. Truscott trilled, her eyes making a rapid inventory. 'So nice to meet you.

But you'll have to come and see me properly . . . perhaps when you're visiting your friends next?'

'Thank you very much, Mrs. Truscott,' Gareth answered formally for both of them. 'That's kind of you.'

'Well, I'd better get on. The girls are waiting for me. We're having a bridge game.' She grated the gears of her car, grimaced and tried again. 'Don't forget,' she called, waving. 'You must come soon.'

'Sorry about that,' Gareth said, moving his car forward. 'I suppose we'd better call in and say hello sometime.'

'Must we?'

'No.' He glanced at her. 'But she lost her husband a year or two ago, and I guess the poor old thing's a bit lonely. I hardly know her myself, but it was kind of her to ask us.'

Yes, it was, Jess supposed. Gareth was really a much nicer person than herself.

Claire did look marginally better. Scott had engaged a nurse to look after her in the daytime, and she was eating properly again and resting a lot, to build up her strength for the operation. Refusing to stay in bed, she sat with her feet up on a sofa in the lounge and talked to them. 'I was only allowed to get up if I let Scott carry me, though,' she said, grimacing.

'You know what the doctor said yesterday—total bed rest. He's worried about the swelling in your ankles,' Scott reminded her.

'They're better already,' Claire said. 'Look, you'd hardly notice, now. I'm sure I could have walked from the bedroom.'

'Stop arguing,' Scott advised curtly. 'I'm not letting

you walk anywhere until the doctor gives you permission, so you may as well give in.'

Claire turned away from him to ask after Jess's father, and Scott sat rather wearily in one of the chairs from where he could see his wife's face.

The date of the operation was fixed for the following week, and Claire seemed certain of a good outcome, happily predicting that after it was over she would be running up and down stairs again without any ill effects and, most important, be able to care for her baby herself. Jess told her the date of the wedding and she said firmly, 'I'll be there. I suppose we'll have to get a babysitter.'

Gareth teased her a little, and Claire laughingly appealed for support from Jess, while Scott sat for the most part in silence, watching the changing expressions on Claire's face, his own showing the strain of the past few weeks. Once he went over to rearrange the cushions behind her back when they began to slip, and Claire said, 'It's all *right,* Scott; don't fuss!'

His mouth tightened, but he said nothing, merely jerking the cushion into place and returning to his seat.

When he got up to go and make coffee for them, Jess followed him into the kitchen, offering to help.

'I can manage,' he said, 'but stay and talk, anyway. I'm glad your father's going to recover, Jess. It must be a big relief for you.'

'Yes. It was odd, going back. It was a sort of reconciliation, too, in a way. I'm not good at them, really.'

He said, 'Neither are we, apparently.'

'You and Claire? Are things still . . . difficult?'

'She won't talk to me, Jess. I mean, really talk.

Please and thank you and yes-it's-a-nice-day. But she never looks at me if she can avoid it, and she's edgy, you can see that. The doctors tell me that irritability is sometimes part of the illness, but . . . I think she hates me.'

'Oh, Scott, no! She feels hurt, that's all. She thinks you let her down. It doesn't mean she hates you.'

'She can't bear to have me touch her,' he burst out bitterly. 'You don't know how that feels . . . especially after . . . It was so different before, even when we knew she was pregnant. Making love with Claire was like nothing else. She was so wholehearted, spontaneous, giving—and never, ever wanting to take precautions, but wanting my baby. I can't describe how it made me feel, that kind of special receptiveness. And she's so . . . Well, it was always good . . . for both of us.'

'But, Scott, surely now you can't . . .'

'No, of course not! I wouldn't dream of asking her. But a touch, a kiss, being able to hold her hand now and then . . . that wouldn't harm her. Only she doesn't want it. She hasn't touched me voluntarily since that day in Dr. Barton's consulting room, and when I kiss her she turns her cheek to me like a submissive Victorian wife doing her duty.'

'Can't you talk about it?'

'I daren't. She's not to be upset, and I'd upset her if I started.'

He wrenched the lid off a jar of instant coffee, scowling as he spooned some of the dark aromatic powder into cups.

Jess said thoughtfully, 'You're not just hurt, are you? You're angry about it, too.'

'I've tried not to be, but I can't help it. I'm trying to make allowances for her illness and the strength of her religious convictions. But I'm being punished for loving her, and it feels bloody unfair. If she wasn't so sick I'd want to shake her into admitting it.'

Hesitantly Jess said, 'Give her time, Scott. Perhaps when the baby comes . . .'

'Perhaps when the baby comes she'll have someone else to love.'

'You're not jealous, are you?'

Scott leaned suddenly on the table, fists closed, his head bowed. 'I don't know anymore. I don't think so. Claire suggested that, too. Maybe I am. I certainly resented the thought of her being so willing to put her own life on the line for the baby.' Straightening with an effort, he picked up the kettle, poured hot water into the cups and said tiredly, 'Pass over that tray, will you, and the sugar?'

'I could try and talk to her,' Jess offered hesitantly, wanting to help but reluctant to interfere.

'It probably wouldn't do any good. She's made up her mind that I'm a cold-blooded child murderer, and that's it.'

He put two cups on the tray with the sugar, milk and some biscuits and picked it up, saying, 'Can you bring the others?'

Gareth had shifted to sit on the side of the sofa, one hand on the back of it. Claire lay back against the cushions, smiling up at him. They made a cosy, almost intimate picture, and Jess, flashing a glance at Scott, thought he was distinctly put out by it.

Gareth turned his head as they entered, rising unhurriedly to take a cup from Jess and resume his erstwhile seat in one of the armchairs.

The conversation became desultory, and Scott said, 'Time for bed, Claire. You're looking tired.'

She seemed about to protest, but Jess said, 'Yes, you are. And I've had a long day, too. We'll be going soon.'

Claire let Scott pick her up in his arms, her hands linking behind his neck. 'Come along and talk to me while I get ready for bed, Jess,' she said. 'Good night, Gareth.'

Scott carried her to their bedroom and lowered her carefully onto the bed while Jess followed and stood just inside the doorway. His hand still behind Claire's back, Scott said, 'Lean forward and I'll unzip you.'

'Jess can help me this time,' Claire said. 'You won't mind, will you, Jess? You go back to the sitting room and talk to Gareth,' she suggested to Scott.

'*Lean forward,*' Scott said. 'Jess can't carry you to the bathroom.' His control slipping, he added, 'I know you'd rather have anyone but me to help you, but you'll just have to put up with it. Close your eyes and pretend it's . . . someone else. You never look at me, anyway.'

'Well, maybe now you know how it feels,' Claire said, her bitter tone a match for his. She threw her head back, gazing at him with bright, resentful eyes.

'How what feels?' he demanded, his hands falling away from her as he straightened.

'Being treated like some sort of nonperson,' she said. 'Someone whose feelings and opinions don't matter.'

'I have never treated you like that!'

'No?' Her voice rose and she laughed, a high-pitched, artificial sound. 'You treated me *exactly* like that, the day your incompetent Dr. Barton said I might "need" an abortion. You didn't listen to me; you didn't even *look* at me—not once! You just sat there and agreed with everything that man said and promised him that you would make sure that I'd have my baby "terminated."'

'It wasn't like that!'

'Yes, it was!' Claire said viciously. 'I was there, and *I* was the one being ignored while you and that beastly man made your rotten arrangements! Without taking any notice of me at all, without once asking me what I thought or how I felt, without even *looking* at me!'

Scott's mouth tightened, and he passed a hand over his eyes. 'Claire,' he said in anguished tones, 'I *couldn't* look at you. I didn't dare. I couldn't bear to see in your face what I was feeling, and what I knew you were feeling even more.' His voice shook. 'Don't you understand? I'd have broken down and howled with grief for you—and for our baby.'

Jess, standing forgotten by the door, held her breath. Claire was staring at her husband with a mixture of incredulity, suspicion and dawning comprehension. 'But you,' she said uncertainly, 'you were so determined I would have the abortion if they thought I should. You said you'd make sure I did. . . .'

'Darling, I can't say I wouldn't have tried. I guess . . . I *know* it was wrong, I should have left the decision to you, let you take the risk if you were willing to—Jess said it was your right—but I still can't promise that I'd act differently if it happened again. I don't know if I could.' He dropped to his knees suddenly beside the bed and caught one of her hands in his. 'Claire, I was terrified that you'd die. I'd have sacrificed anything for your life—anything. Can't you forgive me . . . for loving you?'

Claire was as still as a statue, her face showing an odd

blankness. Scott laid his forehead on her hand, clasped in his, and in a muffled, pleading voice, spoke her name.

Jess backed quietly out of the room, pulling the door closed just as Claire raised her free hand and placed it gently on her husband's bent head.

Chapter Thirteen

The minister didn't look disapproving when Jess admitted that she rarely attended any church, merely saying that they both might like to come more often after their marriage. 'Some people,' he added with a smile, 'find that coping with the marriage relationship demands a little extra help.'

'Do you think we'll need extra help?' she asked Gareth later, as they sat in his flat drinking coffee and listening to a recording of operatic overtures.

'I will need all the help I can get'—he grinned—'with you.'

She made a face at him and put down her cup, kicking off her shoes to curl her long legs up on the sofa.

'That's gorgeous,' she said about the music, and closed her eyes, humming a few bars along with the trumpets.

'We have more in common than you thought, don't we?' he asked her.

Opening her eyes, she regarded him consideringly. 'You could be right.' They both liked good music, read many of the same books, and enjoyed a lively argument about topical issues; and although he didn't share her passion for history, he had a mild interest in the past and knew something about the subject.

'Tell me about your work,' she said.

He laughed. 'Spoken like a dutiful fiancée. You'd be bored rigid.'

Her eyes sparking, she said. 'How do you know? Tell me.'

'Well,' he said, 'I can't use names, but . . .'

He talked about contract work, about negotiations, concessions, writing in protective clauses at the last minute and trying to push them though, frantic phone calls between client and lawyer and the lawyer for the other party, about deals and counterdeals.

'I had no idea,' she said, 'that it could be so complicated. You make it sound like high-level diplomacy.'

'Sometimes it is. Especially when millions of dollars are changing hands. The future of an entire company or conglomerate can hang in the balance. Good contract lawyers, let me tell you, are much in demand.'

'And you're good.'

'Is that a question or a statement?'

'I think it's a statement.'

'That's a remarkably equivocal way of putting it.'

'All right then. You're good. I know it. You'd be good at anything you really wanted to do.'

To her surprise, he coloured a little. 'Thank you, Jess,' he said and picked up her hand in his, looking at the flashes of light and colour in the ring he had given her. He touched it with his finger. 'I'm not accustomed to receiving compliments from you.'

'I'm not accustomed to giving them.'

'My mother wants us to come to a dinner party she's giving on Thursday. Is that all right?'

'Thursday? I think so. It's the day Claire has her operation, but . . . well, yes, I suppose so.'

'It'll all be over by evening, won't it?'

'Yes, surely. I hope everything goes well for her.'

'Scott will let you know, won't he?'

'Yes, he promised. And I'll tell you as soon as I hear from him.'

The record stopped, and Gareth got up and switched off the player. 'Ready to go home?' he asked her.

'Want to get rid of me?'

'Not at all. I just want to remove myself from temptation—or the other way round. What I want to do to you doesn't bear description.'

'I'll get a taxi,' she offered.

'No, we'll take my car. But you can drive. You need the practice.'

She was a reasonably competent driver now, and Gareth seemed to have no qualms about her taking the wheel. He encouraged her to drive as much as possible, and if she didn't enjoy it, at least she had got over her initial fear.

He walked her to the door and kissed her good night, his lips at first gentle, then hard and demanding. 'Have you any idea what this waiting is doing to me?' he muttered in her ear as his hands brought her close to his body.

'Yes,' she said. 'The same as it's doing to me.'

Reluctantly he laughed. 'And you still want to . . . ?'

She was silent for long moments, then eased herself apart from him, so that his hands slid to her hips and rested there lightly. 'Yes,' she said. 'I still want to.'

'All right, all right.' He took his hands away and held them in the air. 'There. Willpower, see?'

'I'm all admiration,' she said and kissed him passionately and briefly on the mouth, laughing as she scooted inside the door and shut it in his face. The wooden panels muffled the sound of his voice, but she would have taken a bet that what he was saying was less than complimentary.

On Thursday she found it difficult to concentrate on her work. She kept looking at the clock—Claire's operation was scheduled for ten that morning—and every time the phone rang she jumped to answer it. The first time it was someone conducting a telephone survey for a flooring manufacturer, and an hour later a wrong number. At twelve Mrs. Seymour was on the line, apparently just to say she was looking forward to seeing Jess that evening. 'I'm looking forward to it, too,' Jess lied politely, only half listening to the older woman's tranquil recitation of who the other guests were. She finally figured out that her future mother-in-law was merely doing the correct thing, making the invitation personal because it had originally been issued through Gareth. Perhaps Jess was also being subtly warned to be on her best behaviour. Apparently the guest list included a prominent judge and some people called 'Sir Thomas' and his lady, whoever they might be.

'Thank you for ringing,' Jess said as soon as she could decently interrupt the flow. 'I'll see you tonight, Mrs. Seymour.'

It wasn't until one o'clock that she finally heard Scott's voice when she picked up the receiver. 'She's still in the theatre,' he said. 'This is the earliest they said to enquire, and there's no news yet. I'll get in touch again when I hear anything. I'd like to be there, but they said there's no point.'

At three o'clock Jess gave up trying to work and phoned Scott's number. There was no reply. She was pacing the floor, imagining all kinds of disasters, when the phone went again.

Snatching up the handset, she barely gave Scott time to open his mouth before she said, 'Is she all right?'

'They say so,' he told her. 'I'm at the hospital; I came with Pietro as soon as she was out of the theatre. The operation was a success; everything went fine; she's holding her own. They let us see her for half a minute. Jess'—his voice wobbled—'she looks so . . . I don't know if she can . . . I'm staying here. Pietro's going home to the boys.'

'Will you be able to sit with her?'

'No, she's in the intensive care unit and they don't allow visitors. I'd be in the way. But I can wait outside, and I made them promise that when she regains consciousness they'll call me.'

'It could be a long wait,' she guessed.

'Yes, so they tell me.'

'Look,' she said, 'I can't work, anyway. Would you like me to come down and keep you company?'

'Jess . . .' His voice softened with emotion. 'I can't ask you to . . .'

'Who's asking?' she demanded. 'I'm on my way.'

She called a taxi and tried to get Gareth at his office, only to be told he wasn't in. She would have to ring again from the hospital.

When she appeared Scott hugged her closely without speaking, and she knew she had done the right thing. He looked haggard as he said, 'Her blood pressure is too low. They're trying to stabilise it.'

'Have you seen her again?'

He shook his head. 'It's all I can do to get any real information from them.'

'Have you eaten anything?' she asked him.

'No. Yes, breakfast, I think. What's the time?'

'Long past lunchtime. I'll see if I can get you a sandwich and some coffee.'

'I don't really want . . .'

'It isn't what you want, it's what you need. I won't be long.'

She found a canteen and made her way back to him with some sort of a meal, which he ate while she stood over him. She had also found a phone booth and tried Gareth's number again. He still wasn't in, but she left a message for him.

Just after five Scott managed to buttonhole a doctor who admitted that Claire was not breathing well on her own and that they had put her on oxygen. Scott went grey. 'Don't worry too much, Mr. Carver,' the doctor went on. 'There's no reason to suppose that anything is seriously wrong. She's been through a very traumatic operation, and her recovery is a little slower than we'd like, that's all.'

After the doctor had left them, Jess glanced at Scott's ashen face and then at her watch and came to a decision. 'I have to make a phone call,' she told him. 'Will you be all right for a while?'

'Yes, of course. Jess, you don't have to stay . . .'

'I'm staying,' she said firmly. 'I won't be long.'

She phoned Gareth at home and this time he answered. 'How is she?' was his first question, and she relayed to him all she knew.

'I'm staying here with Scott,' she said. 'I'm sorry about your mother's dinner party, Gareth. Please apologise for me.'

'Yes, I will,' he promised.

'Gareth?' She hesitated.

'What is it, Jess?'

'You do understand, don't you?'

'Yes,' he said gently. 'I understand perfectly.'

Pietro was back before a smiling nurse came hurrying up to Scott and said, 'You can speak to her for just a second, Mr. Carver. She's awake and breathing on her own.'

When he came back his face still showed strain and his eyes were suspiciously shiny, but the grimness about his mouth had relaxed. 'She looks better,' he said, 'and they tell me the worst is probably over. She's doing well now.'

'Thank God for that,' Jess said. 'You should go home and get some sleep, Scott.'

'Yes, I suppose so.' He looked down at his hands and laughed unsteadily. 'I'm shaking . . . relief, I suppose.'

'I'll drive you home,' she said, watching him swaying on his feet. 'You're in no fit condition . . .'

'You've done enough . . .'

'I'll drive you,' she repeated. 'Where's your car?'

In the end he let her, too tired, she guessed, to argue, and when she had parked his car in the driveway of his home she made him coffee and an omelette and insisted he go to bed.

'What will you do?' he asked her. 'It's . . . God, it's nearly two o'clock.'

'I'll borrow your spare bed if you've got one,' she said. It was a long way back to her place, and she didn't feel like facing the journey. Besides, she wanted to be on hand just in case there was more word from the hospital.

'Yes, of course,' Scott said. 'I don't know if it's made up, but there are sheets. . . .'

'I'll find them. Go to bed,' she said firmly.

She slept well, but woke early all the same. Scott was already up and had made breakfast for them.

'I phoned the hospital,' he said as she appeared in the kitchen. 'She's had a restful night; her blood pressure is almost normal, and I can visit her properly this afternoon for a little while.'

'Oh, good, I'm so glad.'

'Jess,' he said, taking her hand for a moment as they sat down, 'I'm terribly grateful for what you've done. There are times when having no family is tough. I don't know how I'd have made it through this without you.'

'You'd have done it for me,' she said. 'That's what friends are for.'

'Will Gareth mind?'

'Gareth doesn't mind. I spoke to him last night.'

'Well, I'm grateful to him, too. Tell him so, will you?'

'You don't need to be. He doesn't own me, Scott.'

Scott laughed. 'Always the independent woman, aren't you, Jess? Gareth must be quite a guy, to pin you down.'

After breakfast he said, 'I'll pay for a taxi for you, Jess. I don't want to leave the house myself, in case the hospital . . .'

'Yes, I know,' she said swiftly. 'I'll get my own taxi, though.'

'No,' he insisted. 'Let me at least do that, Jess.'

She smiled and submitted. When the taxi came, he went with her out to the pavement and kissed her, holding her for a moment to say, 'Thanks again, Jess. On Claire's behalf, too.'

'Let me know when she's allowed other visitors?' she asked, and he said, 'Sure. Of course.'

She didn't even notice Mrs. Truscott standing at her gate with a milk bottle in her hand as the taxi swept past.

She phoned Mrs. Seymour to apologise in person for missing the dinner, and found her distantly sympathetic. 'Yes, Gareth explained about your sick friend, and as she has no family of her own . . . How is she now?'

'They don't say much,' Jess explained, 'but she's expected to recover.'

'Oh, that's good. Perhaps you and Gareth might like to come for lunch on Saturday? As you missed our little dinner . . .'

'Thank you,' Jess said. 'That would be very nice.'

Mrs. Seymour somehow had that effect on people, she thought, as the conventional phrase left her tongue. It wasn't insincere, really; she liked Karunja, enjoyed the spacious and mellow atmosphere of the house with its historic associations, and loved the garden with its view of the river. And she liked Gareth's father a lot. But there seemed no way to get close to his mother. Mrs. Seymour, in spite of her frequent invitations, her habit of calling Jess 'dear,' her smiling willingness to regale her future daughter-in-law with the history of Gareth's family and his home, and her cultured knowledge of music, art and literature, never became real to Jess. She was like a breathing, talking marble statue.

At lunch on Saturday she said, 'I was saying to Gareth that it would be nice to have the reception here at Karunja after your wedding. He says it's up to you to say, dear. We would like it very much, and as your parents don't live in Sydney . . .'

Glancing at Gareth, Jess got no help. She could only guess that he would probably find the idea attractive. She knew he was fond of Karunja, and certainly it would be an ideal setting. 'Well, that would be very nice,' she said. 'If it's not a lot of trouble.'

'Of course not.' Mrs. Seymour seemed genuinely pleased, and Jess felt a pang of guilt. 'And your parents, Jess . . . Gareth said that you're hoping they will be able to travel down by then. They must stay with us. I haven't seen your little home, but I believe that it's quite tiny, and we can't have them putting up at a hotel.'

'You're very kind,' Jess said, bowed under these coals of fire, 'but they wouldn't want to impose. . . .'

'Nonsense, we have plenty of room. Of course they must come here. If you give me the address, I'll write and ask them properly. Now I don't suppose you're wearing white, dear, but have you thought about attendants at all?'

'No attendants,' Jess said firmly, assailed by visions of a retinue of girlish relatives of Mrs. Seymour's in pink organdy and frills. 'We thought a very simple ceremony.'

'Well, perhaps that is best . . .' Hearing the phrase 'in the circumstances' hanging in the air, Jess caught Gareth's eye and he came gallantly to the rescue.

'Want a game of tennis after lunch, Jess?' he enquired blandly. 'After all, you need to keep your figure trim for the big day, don't you?'

'There's nothing wrong with Jess's figure,' his father remarked.

'I'm aware of that, Dad,' Gareth answered. 'I wouldn't change an inch of it.'

'Gareth,' his mother objected, 'it's not in the best of taste to make embarrassing remarks about your fiancée.'

'Are you embarrassed, Jess?' he asked her.

'Your mother is, on my behalf,' she retored, 'and it's **he**r table and her house.'

'Mother'—Gareth turned to her with exaggerated humility—'I apologise.'

'Oh, go on with you!' she said, and Jess was startled to see the fond look she gave him even as she tried to make it full of reproof.

'I'm sorry if Mother put you in a spot over this reception business,' Gareth said as they walked to the court. 'Do you mind?'

'Not if your mother really wants to do it.'

'Of course she does. It's the kind of thing she enjoys immensely. She's a terrific hostess. Everything runs like clockwork at Mother's "dos."'

'Gareth, will you want me to . . . have dinner parties and things?'

'Only if you want to,' he said. 'Do you like giving parties?'

'Well, it depends. My kind of party tends to be pretty informal.'

'Then that's the kind we'll have. Now, which end of the court do you want?'

Claire's recovery was remarkably swift, once the first few somewhat anxious days had passed. When Jess was allowed to visit her she found her sitting up in bed, a sparkle in her eyes and a healthy colour to her skin.

'I feel better already,' she said. 'And they're even letting me out of bed. By the end of the week I'll be walking the length of the corridor.'

She had an incentive, of course. She was a model patient because she was determined to be fit and healthy for the arrival of her baby. And Jess was very relieved to see that when Scott came into the room her face lit up and she held out her arms to him and lifted her mouth for his kiss.

In the event, Claire stayed in hospital until her transfer to the maternity ward. The baby decided to put in a slightly early appearance, a small but healthy boy, and Scott, when he phoned Jess with the news, was almost incoherent with relief. 'She came through it with flying colours,' he reported. 'Everything's fine. Mother and baby doing perfectly, the doctor says.'

'And in plenty of time for your wedding,' Claire told them when Gareth and Jess visited her again. 'I've had a new dress waiting since I was *this big.* . . .' She stretched her arms round an imaginary pregnancy bulge. 'And it's going to be so nice to be able to fit into it!'

A few days later Mrs. Seymour issued what Jess couldn't help thinking of as a royal summons for her to appear at Karunja and 'go over some of the details for the reception.'

'I can't imagine why,' Jess said to Gareth rather crossly. She had hoped to have the whole week free to get on with her writing. The plot was at a crucial stage and she had set herself a target of two more chapters before the wedding. 'Your mother has everything well in hand, and I'm sure she doesn't need my advice.'

'It's your wedding,' he reminded her. 'She just wants to make sure you're happy with the arrangements.'

'Yes,' she said, feeling like a worm and an ungrateful one at that. 'She's being very generous, Gareth, and I do appreciate the work she's putting into all this, although . . .'

'Although you'd just as soon have done without the reeption, I know,' he said patiently. 'So would I, to tell the truth, but there are certain conventions to be observed, and I don't suppose it will hurt us to fall in with them.'

'Oh, well,' she said. 'When do we go?'

'Any evening this week, Mother said. She also indicated that my presence isn't necessary. I'll drive you there, though, and see if I can persuade my father to give me a game of chess to pass the time while you women are conferring.'

Perhaps the planning had been more of a strain than anyone realised, Jess thought on Wednesday evening when they arrived at Karunja. Mrs. Seymour seemed unusually tense, and Jess told herself with compunction that although she had not asked Gareth's mother to organise a formal reception, she had accepted the offer and might have done more to help.

Determined to remedy the omission, she readily accepted Mrs. Seymour's invitation to join her in the library where she kept the guest list and other notes, while the men had their game of chess in the small sitting room.

Mrs. Seymour went to the little Victorian writing desk in one corner and took out a gold pencil and a notebook in an embossed leather folder, while Jess stood by the table in the centre of the room.

When they were both seated at the table, Jess waited for the other woman to open the notebook, but instead she sat fiddling with the pencil, her motions oddly nervous. 'Jess, dear,' she said finally, 'I wonder if first we could have a little talk.'

Chapter Fourteen

*H*er heart sinking, Jess resisted the urge to ask, About the birds and bees? and tried to look suitably receptive and obliging.

Mrs. Seymour cleared her throat. 'I'm very fond of my children, Jess. I may not show it a lot, our family has never been demonstrative, but . . . well, I have always tried to do my best for them, and even though they are both adults now, as a mother I still care about their welfare and their . . . their happiness.'

'I'm sure you do,' Jess murmured, feeling that the silence following this speech called for some sort of comment, and wondering where it was leading.

'Yes, well, I understand that . . . things . . . are not as they were when I was your age, and that you are a . . . what is called, I suppose, a liberated young woman. But Gareth has, I must warn you, certain principles. He's not a boy anymore, of course, and I dare say there may have been . . . episodes . . . in his life which are best forgotten. But I'm . . . well, I'm quite certain he would not condone any hint of promiscuity in his wife.' Jess blinked as this last sentence came out in a little rush, after which Mrs. Seymour shut her lips tightly, her gaze on the tabletop in front of her.

Keep calm, Jess told herself. She thinks she's doing this for Gareth; she's his mother; she's just got some wild ideas about liberated, divorced women. Quite quietly, she said, 'Mrs. Seymour, I'm not promiscuous. I promise you, I'll be a faithful wife.'

'Yes, well . . . I certainly hope so,' Mrs. Seymour said unhappily. 'I don't want to make any trouble, that's why I thought if I just talked to you privately . . .'

'Well then, I hope I've set your mind at rest,' Jess said crisply.

'Not . . . not quite.' The pencil in Mrs. Seymour's fingers dropped with a small clatter to the table and she put her hand over it, the blue veins prominent. A slight flush appeared on her cheeks. 'You see, there is something that I find . . . Well, for Gareth's sake, I feel I must insist on some sort of . . . of discussion with you. I would never condemn anyone unheard, you must understand that, but on the face of it, Jess, it does appear that you have been, at least, shall we say, unwise?'

'Unwise?' Floundering, Jess looked at her with total incomprehension. 'I'm sorry; I don't understand.'

'I expect you've forgotten that Flora Truscott lives in the same street as your . . . friend, Mr. Carver.'

Thrown by this apparent change of subject, Jess said, 'What?'

The red flush on her cheeks deepening, Mrs. Seymour repeated with great clarity, 'Flora Truscott . . .'

'Oh, yes, your bridge-playing friend,' Jess recalled with something like relief. She hadn't a clue what this conversation was all about, but at least she had made that connection. 'I remember now.'

'Yes, well, Flora rang me a few days ago. She had been extremely troubled and didn't know whether she should, as she put it, 'interfere,' but she finally decided, after thinking about it for some time, that I was entitled to know . . . and she left it to me to decide what ought to be done.'

'Entitled to know what?'

'Well, that . . . that she had seen you leaving Mr. Carver's house early in the morning . . . the morning, actually, after you were supposed to have been at the hospital with your "sick friend." And she had every reason to believe that you had spent the night there alone with him.'

'What reasons?' Jess demanded coldly, beginning to simmer.

Mrs. Seymour touched her lips fastidiously with the tip of her tongue. 'Flora doesn't sleep well since her husband died, and she's only two doors down. She heard Mr. Carver's car come in very late and the sound of voices. She knew his wife was away, she assumed it was to have her baby. In fact she thought the woman's voice might have been his wife's mother, she said.'

'What?' Jess blinked. Claire didn't have a mother.

'Well, if she'd had the baby her mother might have come from . . . I don't know'—the older woman began to look flustered—'somewhere else, wherever she lived, to be with her daughter. Flora thought . . .'

'Flora seems to have done an awful lot of thinking!' Jess snapped.

'Jess, I'm sorry to do this, but for Gareth's sake I feel I must ask you for an explanation. If you were with this man that night . . .'

'Oh, I was with him,' Jess said clearly, her head up and her eyes throwing fire. 'All night. But I don't owe you any explanations, Mrs. Seymour.'

'Perhaps not,' Mrs. Seymour acknowledged stiffly, 'but I do feel that you owe Gareth one. Unless you are asking me to believe that he knows about this . . . incident.'

'No,' Jess said, her cheeks burning with temper. 'He doesn't know because I didn't think it was important enough to mention. But I'll bet you're just dying to tell him.'

'Now, Jess. . . .' The other woman's eyes swivelled nervously as Jess stood up, pushing back her chair so that it rocked.

'I think you should,' Jess said. 'Don't you? Why not right now?'

'Jess!' Mrs. Seymour bleated weakly behind her as she swept out of the room and down the passage to burst in on Gareth and his father, who looked up, startled, from the chessboard.

'What is it?' Gareth asked, getting to his feet.

Jess heaved a deep breath into her chest, forcing herself to speak calmly. 'I'm sorry to disturb your game,' she said, 'but would you mind coming to the library for a few minutes, Gareth? There's something that . . . apparently . . . you ought to know.'

Puzzled, he said, 'What? Well, all right. Excuse me, Dad.'

Jess stalked into the library with him and shut the door. Mrs. Seymour was standing uncertainly by the table, clasping her hands as if she would have liked to wring them. 'Really, Jess,' she said feebly, 'there's no need for this. . . .'

'I think there is,' Jess said succinctly. 'Gareth, your mother has something to say to you. Go on,' she encouraged the other woman, her voice dangerously level. 'Tell him.' Then she walked over to the long window and stood staring into the darkness ouside as though what was happening in the room had nothing to do with her.

She heard Gareth say, 'Mother? Have you two been quarrelling? Because if so, I don't think I . . .'

'Be quiet, Gareth, and listen!' Jess advised crisply, her back still to them.

'Okay, Mother,' he said after a moment. 'What is it?'

'I only asked for an *explanation,*' his mother said defensively, 'but Jess insisted. . . . I gave her every chance to confide in me, and she has admitted . . .'

'Admitted what?'

'Well, it seems that . . . that the night of my dinner party, when Jess was supposed to be at the hospital . . . remember . . . ? You told us she'd phoned and said she was there with a friend who was having an operation. . . .'

'Yes, I remember,' Gareth said impatiently. 'So?'

'Well, Flora says she spent the night with a Mr. Carver who lives in her . . . in Flora's street. But Jess has assured me she is not . . . she isn't in the habit of . . . the thing is, I'm not saying it's happened before,' she added hastily.

Jess's anger boiled over. Swinging round, she fixed

furious eyes on Gareth's mother and said, 'Oh, if it hasn't, it wasn't for lack of trying! There's something else I suppose you should know, Gareth. Not so long ago I told Scott Carver I loved him and asked him to stay the night with me! A pity your mother's little friend wasn't on the scene then!' She flung up her head to stare defiantly at him and was stopped short by the expression on his face.

Turning to his mother, he said, 'I think this is between me and Jess, Mother. Would you mind leaving us alone for a while?'

He opened the door for her punctiliously, and shut it quietly before turning to face Jess.

'That wasn't true,' she blurted out, shaken to the core by the austere bleakness of his face. 'At least, it was, but not the way I made it sound. . . .'

'It's all right, Jess. I know how you feel about Scott. I just hope for all our sakes that, as Claire's almost well again, you'll let her do any comforting he needs from now on.'

'You said you didn't mind my staying with Scott at the hospital. . . .'

'Not quite true. I tried not to.'

'You said you understood!'

'I did. All too well. And I know you didn't sleep with him, that night or any other.'

'How do you know?' Her voice went hard. 'Your mother . . .'

'My mother doesn't know you as I do. For one thing, you'd never have done that to Claire. . . .'

'Or you!' she said swiftly.

After a moment he said, 'Or me. And if you had yielded to temptation, you'd have told me, probably the next day, certainly before now.'

'There was no temptation!' she said. 'Gareth, you don't still think that I'm in love with Scott, do you?'

He looked at her levelly. 'Aren't you?'

For a few moments she was speechless. 'I *told* you!' she said.

'Yes, you did, smiling through your tears like a true little heroine,' he said. 'I didn't believe you.'

'Well, it's time you did! I am not, and never have been, in love with Scott Carver! I *love* him, in much the same way that I love Claire. Not at all like . . .'

'Like what?' he asked quietly, his eyes suddenly very intent.

'Well,' she muttered, her eyes sliding away from his as she made a small, deprecating gesture with her hand and her shoulder, 'like I love you, of course.'

Almost curiously, he asked, 'Do you really mean that?'

Exasperated, she glared at him. 'Of course I mean it! Why on earth do you think I'm marrying you?'

He shrugged. 'Second best,' he said, still looking at her as though not quite believing what she said. 'You couldn't have Scott, and there was this . . . something between us, so . . .'

'Oh, thanks!' she said. 'Since when did you decide I'm a person who will settle for second best? And while we're on the subject, what about you and Claire?'

'What about Claire?' he asked warily.

'Well, you told me you wanted to marry her. . . .'

'Not exactly. I said I might have asked her. . . .'

'If Scott hadn't come along. Well, were you going to ask her to marry you without being in love with her?'

He looked slightly discomfited. 'Yes, actually,' he said. 'I'd decided I wasn't likely to fall in love again like the first time. I liked Claire a lot and she seemed to feel the same about me. She's very attractive, and she reminded me sometimes of Angela. I was thinking about it quite seriously when . . .'

'When Scott came along.'

'No. *You* did.'

'I . . . *I* did? But you admitted you hadn't thought of marrying me until . . .'

'I didn't want to think of it. Only I knew I couldn't ask Claire or anyone else to be my wife as long as I felt the way I did about you.'

'But you didn't want to ask *me*, either.'

He looked at her queerly, and she said, 'Well, you didn't! It's all right; I know I'm not the kind of woman you wanted for a wife. I suppose I ought to be pleased that in the end you overcame your scruples and asked me. Are you sure your mother isn't right, though? A nicely brought up lad like you marrying a woman like me. I'm not suitable material for an up-and-coming lawyer's wife; we both know that. I mean, you can still change your mind. . . .'

'Stop it, Jess!'

'No, I mean it,' she said. 'It's not too late to call it off. . . .'

'You *dare!*' he said, and reached her side in two strides, grabbing her wrists to haul her into her arms.

'But you don't really want . . .'

'*Shut up!*' he said fiercely, and kissed her with ferocious passion until she went fluid and responsive and kissed him back.

When he stopped and looked down at her flushed face, both of them breathing quickly, she said, 'But it's true. You just said you didn't want to think about marrying me. You didn't even *like* me. . . . You were always finding fault with me, criticising.'

'Yes,' he said ruefully, 'I know. And you thought me a self-righteous prig, with some reason. It was a form of self-defence, I think.'

Suspiciously she repeated, 'Self-defence?'

'Look at me,' he said, letting his arms fall away from her to spread his hands wide. 'There you were, a beautiful divorcée, into Pacific cruising with Scott Carver and his friends and evenings out with Pietro Benotti, living on "very generous" maintenance cheques from a filthy rich ex-husband—and here I was, a moderately successful, not very tall, not in the least handsome, dull and undistinguished contract lawyer, so insignificant that the first time we met I was practically *invisible* to you. And when you burst into tears at his wedding reception . . .'

'I did not!' she denied, revolted.

'Started genteelly sniffing, then. Anyway, I was convinced that you were in love with Scott, the guy who has everything—money, a life of glamour and adventure, looks and a physique that any woman would be bowled over by. How was I supposed to compete? I got a tremendous kick when I realised that the attraction wasn't all on my side, that you felt something, too. But you also told me you liked being one of the idle rich, and you certainly didn't seem enamoured of marriage! Of course I tried to find faults in you. I didn't *want* to fall in love with you. All I could see in that was maybe a few weeks of bliss, if I was lucky, before you went off arm in arm with some Scott Carver lookalike who'd kick sand in my face.'

'Actually,' Jess said, 'I happen to think that you're gorgeous.'

He looked at her, and a slow flush spread over his face.

'Well,' she said with a funny little shrug, watching his embarrassed pleasure, 'there's no accounting for taste.'

'I think you're gorgeous, too, Jess,' he said, starting to smile. 'Everything about you . . . your ruthless honesty and your fierce loyalty, your belief in yourself, your courage, your bullheaded pride, your candid passion and your tart sense of humour—even the way you flare up when you're angry, and get snide when you feel threatened, and the way you barge hellbent at problems. I love you, and I want to go on loving you forever. In fact, I don't think I'll be able to help it.'

'Well,' she complained, finding it all a little too much to cope with, 'it's taken you long enough to get round to telling me!'

'What on earth are you talking about now?' he said, folding his arms about her and rubbing his face against her hair.

'What I said,' she told him crossly. 'You've never actually told me that before.'

'I *must* have!'

'Oh, in bed, maybe.'

'Doesn't that count?'

'No. It might have helped if you'd mentioned all this when you proposed, instead of leering at me in that disgustingly sexy way.'

'I'm willing to accept it was sexy, but I'm sure I was never disgusting. Anyway'—he was nibbling on her ear and she tipped her head to let him—'you're eminently leerable.'

'I'm sure there's no such word.'

'There is now; I just invented it.'

'You can't . . .'

'I've never met such a woman for arguing. Shut up and kiss me.'

'You're always telling me . . . Oh, God, Gareth!' She pushed away from him, leaning back on his encircling arms. 'Your mother!'

'My mother?' he said blankly.

'She'll hate me. I lost my temper. And what I said . . . !'

'Maybe she deserved it.'

'She was only thinking of you. Didn't you tell her that night that I was with Scott at the hospital?'

'I didn't want to go into lengthy explanations in front of all the guests, and anyway I suppose I was feeling slightly raw because you had flown to Scott's side. I just said you had a sick friend with no relatives and you were standing by at the hospital. It was all they needed to know.'

'But surely your parents know Claire?'

'No. I never got as far as bringing her home to meet them. That privilege was reserved for you.'

'Well, if she didn't even have enough knowledge to put two and two together, you can't really blame your mother for making five, I suppose,' she offered generously.

'If I were a male chauvinist I'd say that's a piece of typically feminine logic.'

'You are,' she said sweetly, 'and it is. So much more logical than the male kind. Do you think she'll bring herself to forgive me?'

'I think she'll be very relieved if you forgive *her*, seeing as she was totally, horribly wrong, something I will very gently explain. She doesn't give her love easily or show it readily, but once she accepts a person she's very faithful to them. She was extremely fond of Angela—and she's never met anyone like you. Just give her time, Jess.'

'Yes, well, I'd better go and make my peace with her.'

'Hey,' he said, pulling her back as she went to open the door, 'how about making peace with me first?'

'For what?' she asked, linking her hands behind his neck as his arms encircled her waist again.

'I don't know,' he confessed as his head came down and his lips touched hers, 'but I'll think of something.'

She laughed against his mouth and gave herself up without reserve to his kiss.

Silhouette Special Edition. Romances
for the woman who expects a little
more out of love.

If you enjoyed this book, and you're ready for more great romance

...get 4 romance novels FREE when you become a Silhouette Special Edition home subscriber.

Act now and we'll send you four exciting Silhouette Special
Edition romance novels. They're our gift to introduce you to our
convenient home subscription service. Every month, we'll send
you six new passion-filled Special Edition books. Look them
over for 15 days. If you keep them, pay just $11.70 for all six. Or
return them at no charge.

We'll mail your books to you two full months *before they are
available anywhere else.* Plus, with every shipment, you'll receive
the Silhouette Books Newsletter absolutely free. *And with
Silhouette Special Edition there are never any shipping or han-
dling charges.*

Mail the coupon today to get your four free books—and more
romance than you ever bargained for.

Silhouette Special Edition is a service mark and a registered trademark
of Simon & Schuster, Inc.

Enjoy romance and passion, larger-than-life...

Now, thrill to 4 Silhouette Intimate Moments novels (a $9.00 value)— ABSOLUTELY FREE!

If you want more passionate sensual romance, then Silhouette Intimate Moments novels are for you!

In every 256-page book, you'll find romance that's electrifying...involving...and intense. And now, these larger-than-life romances can come into your home every month!

4 FREE books as your introduction.

Act now and we'll send you four thrilling Silhouette Intimate Moments novels. They're our gift to introduce you to our convenient home subscription service. Every month, we'll send you four new Silhouette Intimate Moments books. Look them over for 15 days. If you keep them, pay just $9.00 for all four. Or return them at no charge.

We'll mail your books to you *as soon as they are published.* Plus, with every shipment, you'll receive the Silhouette Books Newsletter absolutely free. *And Silhouette Intimate Moments is delivered free.*

Mail the coupon today and start receiving Silhouette Intimate Moments. Romance novels for women...not girls.

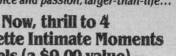
